BLUE MOON

BLUE MOON

JAMES PONTI

ALADDIN

NEW YORK   LONDON   TORONTO   SYDNEY   NEW DELHI

ALADDIN

An imprint of Simon & Schuster Children's Publishing Division
1230 Avenue of the Americas, New York, NY 10020
First Aladdin hardcover edition October 2013
Copyright © 2013 by James Ponti
All rights reserved, including the right of reproduction in whole or in part in any form.
ALADDIN is a trademark of Simon & Schuster, Inc., and related logo is a registered trademark of Simon & Schuster, Inc.
For information about special discounts for bulk purchases, please contact
Simon & Schuster Special Sales at 1-866-506-1949 or business@simonandschuster.com.
The Simon & Schuster Speakers Bureau can bring authors to your live event. For more information or to book an event contact the Simon & Schuster Speakers Bureau at 1-866-248-3049 or visit our website at www.simonspeakers.com.
Designed by Lisa Vega
The text of this book was set in Adobe Garamond Pro.
Manufactured in the United States of America 0813 FFG
10 9 8 7 6 5 4 3 2 1
Full CIP data is available from the Library of Congress
ISBN 978-1-4424-4131-6
ISBN 978-1-4424-4133-0 (eBook)

For Alex and Grayson,
who, in addition to being my sons,
are also my heroes

Acknowledgments

Although this is a work of fiction, it was only made possible by some very real people, many of whom, like the characters in this book, live and work in New York City, but none of whom are actually undead. At least as far as I know.

Despite their aversion to excessive adjective usage, the Omega team at Aladdin is amazing, brilliant, talented, kind, thoughtful, encouraging, and fun. It is led by Fiona Simpson and Bethany Buck, and includes Annie Berger, Craig Adams, Jessica Handelman, and Nigel Quarless.

Speaking of adjectives, only superlatives apply to my agent/friend/confidante Rosemary Stimola, who somehow manages to keep her eye on the smallest detail without losing sight of the big picture, and has done more for lowercase letters than anyone since e.e. cummings.

Suzanne Collins is a remarkable writer, but she's an even better person. I treasure her advice, her generosity, and, most of all, her friendship. I count myself lucky that we are the only two who truly understand and appreciate the Egg Mystery.

Most of all, I want to thank my wife and children, who turn the solitary process of writing into something that is truly a family affair. They inspire, solve, challenge, reassure, and proofread. But most important, they fill my heart every day.

PROLOGUE

Countdown

I've never had much luck when it comes to New Year's resolutions. Last year I only lasted three days before realizing I couldn't survive in a world without junk food. And the year before that, when my sister and I promised not to argue anymore, we didn't even make it to the end of my dad's New Year's Eve party. I'll spare you the gory details, but fruit punch and guacamole were involved. So was dry cleaning.

Here's hoping this year will be more successful. I've skipped the "live healthier" and "live happier" type of resolutions and have settled instead on the just plain "live."

"This year I, Molly Bigelow, resolve to stay alive."

That's it.

I know that sounds fake, like "I won't eat liver" or "I won't get abducted by aliens," but I'm totally serious. In the last five months I've been in eleven different life-or-death situations. Or is it twelve? You'd think I'd know the exact number, right? But it's hard to keep track of them all when you're an Omega.

The Omegas are a secret society responsible for protecting New York City from the undead. It turns out there are zombies all over Manhattan. And while a lot of them hide out underground in abandoned sewers and subway tunnels, even more have lives that seem like yours and mine. (You know, except for the part about breathing.) That's what makes my job so hard. Finding them can be difficult. Despite what you may have seen in horror movies, most zombies look normal.

The two I'm following right now could pass for a hipster couple hanging out in a coffee shop. The girl's wearing skinny jeans and a vintage jacket, and the guy has on a furry hat with earflaps that should be dorky but actually looks kind of cool. There's nothing at all suspicious about them . . . unless you know what to look for.

For example, her jacket is way too light considering it's

already in the low forties and about to get much colder. The undead aren't warm-blooded. They're no-blooded, so temperature doesn't affect them. And he goes out of his way to make sure he never shows his teeth, even when he smiles. A big giveaway for many zombies, because their teeth can turn orange and yellow.

Still, I wouldn't tag them as undead just because of a jacket and a non-smile. After all, she might put fashion before comfort, and he could just be shy. The giveaway was when I spotted them sneaking into the Rockefeller Center subway station from a darkened tunnel that leads to abandoned tracks. You know, as opposed to getting off an actual subway like most people.

I've been tailing them for about five blocks now, and from all appearances they're both Level 2s, which means that in addition to being undead, they have no souls or consciences. This makes them extremely dangerous.

Normally, I try to stay at least a half block away when I'm following someone, but tonight I'm doing my best to keep within fifteen feet because the streets are total chaos. Nearly a million people are trying to cram into Times Square to celebrate New Year's Eve, and if I lose sight of them here I'll never find them again.

Every once in a while, one of the two checks to make

sure they're not being followed and I do my best to blend into the crowd. With all of the people around it's not likely they'd notice me, but I'm still careful not to look right at them. Omega training taught me that it's hard to remember a face if you've never made eye contact.

At Forty-Fifth Street we reach a security checkpoint where the police start herding us like farm animals into barricaded chutes. I almost wind up in the wrong one, but I fight my way against the flow of people and wedge in behind the two suspects.

Eventually, we dead-end into a pen, and once it's full, a policeman puts up another barricade behind us and closes us in. There's no getting in or out for food or bathroom breaks. This is where we're staying for the next four and a half hours until a giant crystal ball drops down a flagpole and signals the start of the New Year. It's a classic New York tradition that dates back to the early 1900s, and the undead have been a part of it since the beginning.

The fact that they've been coming all these years where anyone could see them, yet no one ever has, shows how clever the undead really are. (Another thing the horror movies tend to miss.)

This year, however, it seems as though they may be coming out of hiding and stepping into the spotlight. We know the undead are planning something big for tonight, but we haven't been able to figure out exactly what it is.

That's what has us worried.

All we know for certain is that there are a million people who have nothing to protect themselves with except for noisemakers and paper hats.

And us.

Omegas old and new are scattered throughout Times Square. In fact, there are more Omegas here tonight than have ever been together before. That's because we're determined to make sure everyone else gets a chance to make their resolutions come true too.

I take my spot right behind the couple and wait. They're not going anywhere and neither am I. I have four and a half hours to figure out what their plan is and come up with a way to stop it. That gives me enough time to think back to when this started and try to notice any clues I might have missed along the way.

It all began with the most indestructible zombie ever imagined and a bowlful British candy bars. . . .

Ω 1

Trick or Treat

I mean seriously.

So far this zombie had survived a lead pipe to the head, the total dislocation of his right arm, and a puncture in his stomach that now oozed yellow slime. Yet somehow none of it had slowed him down. He just kept coming right at me doing the wail and flail, which is what we call it when a zombie makes those creepy moaning noises and walks all stiff-legged and jerky. I kept my cool when he flashed the death stare with his milky white eyes. But when he reached out and I saw the chunks of dead flesh dangling from finger bones right in front of my face, I couldn't help myself.

I flinched.

And how did my friends react? How do you think they reacted? They laughed hysterically.

"What?" I asked defensively as I took off my 3-D glasses and realized that I might have done more than flinch.

The zombie was still there, frozen in midsnarl on the giant television screen. Alex, who had just pressed the pause button on the remote, shook his head in total disbelief. "I'm sorry, but aren't you the girl who just defeated Marek Blackwell in an epic battle at the top of the George Washington Bridge?" He pointed at the neon purple cast on my left arm. "Isn't that how you broke your hand?"

"Your point?"

"My point is that you've faced an actual Level 2 zombie," he said. "How can you be frightened by this ridiculous movie?"

"I'm n-not . . . frightened," I said with a stammer even though I was hoping to sound confident. "Why would you even say that?"

"Oh, I don't know," answered Grayson. "Maybe because you went like this." He held his hands in front of his face and cowered as he let out a shriek so ridiculous, I couldn't help but laugh too.

"I guess scary movies scare me," I conceded. "But I didn't squeal. I just *flinched*."

"Keep telling yourself that," Grayson replied.

The truth is I normally avoid scary movies no matter what. It's like a rule for me. But this was no normal situation. Officially our team was dissolved, but we'd managed to petition for a hearing to review the case. For now we were suspended until our fate could be decided. It had been a couple of weeks, and our Omega team was so desperate for any sort of undead action, we were spending Halloween watching a zombie movie marathon in Natalie's apartment. Mostly, we made fun of how fake and unbelievable the movies were. But Natalie's family has a deluxe home theater that's tricked out with a giant 3-D television and surround-sound speakers that make even the cheesiest horror movies seem realistic.

"If you'd like, we can watch some cartoons instead," Alex joked. "Or does it scare you too much when the Road Runner gets the anvil to fall on the Coyote?"

"You are sooooo funny," I replied, mustering all the sarcasm I could manage as I whacked him on the back of the head with a pillow.

That's when Natalie came into the room with a massive bowl of candy. Like they did with everything else, her parents had gone overboard with the Halloween treats.

"Unless there are a couple of hundred kids in the building I don't know about, there's no way we're going to give all of this out tonight," she said as she set it on the table in front of us. "So help yourself to as much as you'd like."

Alex gave the bowl the same look a lion gives a herd of zebras before he quickly began devouring his prey. Grayson, however, picked up a piece and examined its shiny orange wrapper before asking, "What kind of candy is this? I've never even seen it before."

"Well, we just can't have normal candy, can we?" Natalie replied with a phony British accent. "Mum and Dad had to special-order chocolate from England. You know, to impress the neighbors who, by the way, don't have kids and won't ever see it. It's ridiculous."

"It's not ridiculous," Alex mumbled as he tried to talk and chew at the same time. "It's delicious!" He swallowed a bite and announced, "Best. Chocolate. Ever."

"Glad you like it," Natalie said as she settled into the cushy chair next to mine. "So what was that scream I heard when I was in the other room?"

"Grayson trying to be funny," I answered. "And failing epically."

"Not that scream," she corrected. "The one before that."

I slumped.

"*That* was Molly," Grayson said. "Flinching . . . epically."

"She was terrified of him," Alex explained, pointing toward the zombie on the television.

Natalie rolled her eyes. "You can't be serious."

"It's a scary movie!" I reminded them. "You're supposed to get scared watching scary movies. It's considered normal behavior."

"Well, you've only got one more week to be normal," she reminded me. "So get it out of your system."

She didn't need to say anything more than that. I knew exactly what she meant. Our review hearing was set for the following week, and when we presented our case to the panel of past Omegas, we'd have to be much better than normal. We were asking them to lift our suspension, and to do that, we'd need to convince them that we were essential in the fight against the undead. If they ruled against us, our team would most likely be disbanded.

"Is that why you didn't wear a costume?" Grayson asked me. "Because costumes scare you too?"

My lack of a costume had been a running joke all night long. When I arrived at the apartment, I was more than a little surprised to find the others had all dressed for the occasion. Grayson was decked out as a superhero; Alex wore a vampire's cape and plastic fangs; and Natalie went full Bride of Frankenstein, with pancake makeup, a huge wig, and a tattered wedding dress. Meanwhile, I'd come dressed as . . . me.

"Nobody told me we were supposed to wear costumes," I protested.

"It's Halloween," Grayson said. "We kind of figured it was obvious."

(Dear World, when it comes to social situations, what's obvious to you is totally not obvious to me.)

The funny thing is that I was going to wear a costume but decided it would be a big mistake. Since they're all older than me, I assumed they'd outgrown Halloween costumes and that wearing one would make me look too young. I didn't want to be the only one dressed up. So, instead, it turned out that I was the only one not dressed up. Arrgh.

It also didn't help that unlike every previous October of my life, I wasn't really in a Halloween mood. Normally, I spent weeks trying to figure out the perfect costume; but this year it just didn't seem like the thing to do. I'd been in a funk ever since my battle with Marek atop the bridge. This had less to do with the fight and more to do with the fact that I'd been rescued by my mother. That would be the same mother whose funeral I'd attended two and a half years earlier. Once you've discovered that your mom is an actual zombie, dressing up like one doesn't seem like fun.

I haven't told anyone about my mother. I mean, really, what can I say? ("Hey, you know those zombies we're always fighting? Turns out one's my mom!") It's even worse at home. I feel so guilty when I'm around my father and sister, but there's no way to tell them Mom's a resident of Dead City when they have no idea what Dead City is. I'm pretty sure they would call a psychiatrist right around the part where I say, "You see, there are thousands of zombies living underneath New York City. . . ." So I had this huge dilemma, and there was no one I could talk to about it. The only person who could possibly understand would have been . . . my mom. After all, she had been an Omega when she was in school (a legendary one, in fact), and she would be able to help me figure this all out. But she disappeared within moments of saving my life.

I desperately wanted to go down into Dead City to look for her, but I couldn't do that to my friends. *I* was the reason that our team had been suspended, and the three of them had staked their reputations to defend me. If I went underground without permission, it would ruin everything and our suspension would become permanent. So I just had to act like it never happened.

"I'll look for a less scary movie," Alex joked as he started to click through the channels. "Maybe one with rainbows and puppies."

I was about to make a smart-alecky comment when something on the screen caught my eye.

"Wait a second," I said. "Go back."

"Back to the zombie movie?" he asked hopefully.

"No," I replied. "Back to the news."

He flipped back a couple of channels to a local newscast. A reporter with slicked-back hair, professor glasses, and way too much spray tan was sitting at a desk. Behind him was the picture of a man and the headline SUBWAY DEATH.

"I think I know that guy," I said, pointing at the screen. "But I can't remember where I've seen him."

Natalie laughed.

"That's Action News reporter Brock Hampton," she said, doing her best overly dramatic news reporter impression. "Remember? We eavesdropped on his newscast when we went to the crime scene on Roosevelt Island."

I looked at the reporter for a moment and realized she was right. "Hey, that *is* him," I said. "But that's not who I was talking about. I was talking about the dead guy. I've seen *him* somewhere before too."

According to the report, early that morning a man named

Jacob Ellis had been found dead on a subway in Brooklyn, and the police were still trying to determine what had happened. There were two unusual details that made the story newsworthy. One was that his right arm was completely missing. The other was that he was handcuffed to his seat.

"Despite the handcuffs, the police say that Ellis was not an escaped prisoner and, in fact, had never been in trouble with the law," Brock Hampton intoned. "Perhaps it was a Halloween prank gone wrong, or maybe just a case of someone being extremely . . . unlucky."

"Unlucky?" Grayson asked. "I think if you're dead and someone steals your arm, you've gone way beyond being *unlucky*."

"That's it," I said as I grabbed the remote from Alex and froze the image on the screen. I studied the face for a moment. "Jacob Ellis was one of the Unlucky 13."

"The unlucky what?" asked Alex.

"You remember the pictures I found in the *Book of Secrets*?" I asked.

"You mean the ones you weren't supposed to look at or do anything about, but you did anyway, and it led to all of us getting suspended?" asked Natalie. "You mean those pictures?" (She was joking, but there was no denying that she was right.)

15

"Okay, stupid question," I said. "But those pictures were of the men who were killed in the subway tunnel explosion back in 1896. In Dead City they're known as the Unlucky 13. That guy was one of them. He was one of the very first zombies."

Suddenly, Alex was interested. "Are you sure?"

I looked right into the dead man's eyes on the TV screen. "Positive."

"He's been alive for over a hundred and ten years and he just dies on the subway and gets his arm stolen," Grayson said. "There's got to be a story behind that."

Unlike the movie monsters we'd been watching all night, we'd finally caught a glimpse of a real zombie story. Suspended or not, we began to look at the situation like an Omega team.

"Do you think it's like when the three guys pretended to be dead on Roosevelt Island?" Alex asked. "Do you think maybe he's just faking being dead to get back into the morgue?"

"I would," said Grayson. "But his body was discovered in Brooklyn. He's dead dead."

That's the part that didn't make any sense to me. There's no way the undead can survive off Manhattan and away from the Manhattan schist, so why was he in Brooklyn? That's when it hit me. "Maybe that's what killed him."

"Yeah," Alex said, putting it together with me. "Maybe he was on the subway and couldn't get off before it left Manhattan."

Alex, Grayson, and I all said it at the same time: "Because somebody handcuffed him to his seat."

After a few weeks on the sidelines, we'd possibly made a major Dead City discovery. Needless to say, we were a little excited. There may have been high fives and fist bumps.

"That's really something," Alex said as he opened another piece of candy and popped it in his mouth.

Grayson nodded and asked, "But why would someone steal his arm?"

"Stop it," Natalie said, interrupting. "I've seen you guys like this. You've got undead on the brain and you want to figure out what really happened."

"Of course we do," Grayson said.

"When you think about it," added Alex, "it's the perfect way to kill a zombie."

"No, when you think about it, it's the perfect way to ruin our review hearing," she countered. "We have been told to avoid any and all Omega activity, and that's exactly what we're going to do."

"What about Molly? She killed Marek Blackwell on the bridge. And she killed his brother Cornelius in the locker room after her fencing tournament," protested Alex. "That's all Omega activity."

"No," Natalie corrected. "She defended herself and saved her life. It was an extraordinary circumstance."

"Don't you think this is one too?" Grayson asked. "One of the original zombies getting murdered on a subway train sounds pretty extraordinary."

Natalie was having trouble controlling her frustration, so I came to her rescue. "She's right," I said, interrupting. "I'm just as curious as you guys, but we can't jeopardize our hearing."

"But . . . ," Alex said, starting to argue. Both he and Grayson wanted to disagree with us, but in their hearts they knew we were right.

"What about next week?" Grayson asked. "After the review hearing?"

Natalie smiled. "If we get reinstated, we're all over it. But until then, we've got to act like we've never even heard the word 'undead.' We have to prove that we can follow orders."

We slumped back into our seats and tried to get our minds off the situation. We flipped channels for a while and even went back to watching the zombie marathon. But after a glimpse of an actual undead story, a phony one only seemed that much less realistic. This time it didn't even make me flinch. Finally, Natalie had a suggestion.

"Why don't we go watch the Procession of the Ghouls?"

"Really?" Grayson said, a trace of excitement in his voice. "I thought you had to stay here to give out candy."

"We haven't had any trick-or-treaters for a while, so I think we're done for the night," answered Natalie.

"The Procession of the Ghouls would be fun," Alex said in his best Dracula voice. "But all the costumes might scare Molly." He added a silly vampire laugh.

"I think I can handle it," I assured them. "Let's go."

The Procession of the Ghouls is an annual tradition on the Upper West Side, not far from Natalie's apartment building. It features some of the most elaborate costumes you've ever seen and takes place in the Cathedral Church of St. John the Divine, where the huge pipe organ plays scary music.

As we walked down Amsterdam Avenue toward the cathedral, I couldn't help but think that on Halloween, at least, New York looked like an aboveground version of Dead City. There were scary-looking characters everywhere. Add to this the light mist in the air and the occasional howl of the wind rushing between the buildings, and it began to feel a little eerie. Still, after the flinching incident, there was no way I was going to let on that any of this spooked me.

Luckily, Grayson and Alex got too distracted to pay

much attention to me. They were in the middle of a debate about a science-fiction costume that Grayson said was inaccurate.

"The vest is from the original movie," he pointed out. "But the helmet is from the sequel. Wearing them both at the same time doesn't make any sense. It's like a caveman wearing a business suit."

"Now, that would be funny," Natalie said, egging them on.

"What movie the vest is from isn't important; it's obviously still the same character," Alex said. "Why do you have to be such a snob?"

"I'm not a snob," Grayson responded. "I'm just a costume . . . connoisseur."

"Okay." Alex laughed. "The fact that you call yourself a 'costume connoisseur' proves that you're a snob."

As they continued to bicker back and forth, they missed the moment when I really did flinch. Unlike during the movie, which was just a shocked reaction, this one took my breath away. I kept noticing someone in the corner of my eye and began to worry that we were being followed. Then I saw her reflection in a store window and realized that, mixed in with all of the ghosts and goblins, there was an actual zombie about thirty feet behind us.

It was my mother.

2

The Big Bang

My name is Milton Blackwell, and I am 137 years old. During the Civil War, my father fought in the Battle of Gettysburg, and when I was a young boy, I attended the dedication of the Statue of Liberty. I have witnessed New York City's rise from cobblestone streets to concrete canyons. I was here the day that Wall Street crashed in 1929 and the day Times Square flooded with people celebrating the end of World War II. I've seen parades honoring Charles Lindbergh when he flew across the Atlantic and the Apollo astronauts after they returned from the moon. I've been an observer to so much living history, yet always *that—an observer. That's because I'm not truly alive.*

I'm undead. And I'm not alone.

I'm making this video so a record exists that explains how it came to be that Manhattan has both a living and an undead population. But, before I do that, let me state without hesitation that I alone am to blame for everything that went wrong.

Like the universe, it all began with a big bang. On this date, October 31, 1896, I was one of thirteen members of a crew trying to dig New York's first subway tunnel. The crew was composed entirely of my brothers and cousins. We all worked for Blackwell & Sons, a construction company owned by our grandfather. Our foreman was my eldest brother Marek.

If it is possible to both idolize and be terrified of the same person, then that is how I felt about Marek. He was brilliant and brave but also capable of sudden violence and rage.

I learned this when I was nine years old.

At the time, New York was still a city of dirt roads and horse-drawn carriages. One day, a neighborhood boy playing a prank accidentally spooked a horse, causing it to run wild. I had just started crossing the street and could not get out of its way. I was trampled by the horse and dragged by the overturned carriage.

I was unconscious and barely breathing, my bent limbs lying in every direction in the muddy street. Anyone should have assumed that I had no chance to survive. But Marek was not just anyone. And, luckily, he was the first to reach me.

He scooped up my broken body into his arms and ran for over a mile until we reached a house that also served as a small hospital. He chose it not because of its location—others were closer—but because of its history. The infirmary, as it was known, specialized in caring for women and children. More important, it had been founded by the first female doctor in American history.

Her name was Elizabeth Blackwell.

She ran the infirmary with her sister Emily, and, while our relation to them was distant at best, Marek trusted that, unlike other doctors who might see mine as a hopeless cause, family bonds, no matter how slight, would compel them to fight for my survival. To Marek, nothing was stronger than family, and he counted on them feeling the same way.

"He's a Blackwell," I heard him say as I drifted in and out of consciousness. "And he needs you."

Due to my head injuries and the side effects of nineteenth-century medication, I only have a few brief memories from the two and a half months I spent at the infirmary. I can remember waking up on several occasions with Marek at my bedside, squeezing my hand and repeating the mantra, "Blackwells are strong. Blackwells survive." I also remember overhearing one of the doctors tell my parents that Marek's actions had saved my life. But my most vivid memory from the hospital is of the apology I received from the boy who had accidentally riled the horse.

Like me, he had come to the infirmary as a patient. His arm and leg were badly broken, and his left eye was swollen shut. He limped into my room using a small wooden crutch and took a seat next to my bed.

"I am so sorry, Milton," he said earnestly. "I want to make sure you know that it was an accident."

"Of course it was," I answered. "I don't blame you at all."

"Really?" he said as he let out a sigh of relief. "How are you feeling?"

"I'm doing better," I replied. "How about you?"

"I'm also doing better."

We sat there for a moment, and all the while, a question nagged at me. Something just didn't make sense. Finally, I asked him, "How did you get hurt?"

"The same way you did," he replied with a weak smile. "I was trampled by the horse."

Even though my mind was in a fog, this didn't seem possible. My memory of everything up until the moment of the accident was clear, and I was certain that the horse had run away from him and toward me. I tried to figure out how the horse might have doubled back after I was unconscious, but then I realized what had actually happened.

"Marek?" I whispered, sad that I would even think such a thing about my own brother. "Marek did this to you, didn't he?"

The boy's one good eye opened wide with fear, and I knew that I was right. My brother had appointed himself judge and jury and punished him for what happened to me.

"No," he said with a shaky voice that only convinced me that much more that I was right. "It was the horse." Rather than continue our conversation, he scrambled back onto his crutch and hobbled out the door as he said, "I'll let you rest for now and come back some other time."

He never came back, and I rarely saw him around the neighborhood afterward. He faded from memory until years later when we were trying to dig that first subway tunnel. That's when I saw the same fear in the eyes of my brothers and cousins on the crew. All of them were afraid of being the one who might upset or disappoint Marek.

And all of them were counting on me to make sure that didn't happen.

I wasn't supposed to be part of the crew. Many of the injuries I received in the accident were permanent, and I simply wasn't strong enough for such backbreaking work.

Rather than muscle, my value to the family business was to be brainpower. In 1896, when the others started working on the tunnel, I began my third year as a chemistry student at Columbia University.

I wasn't brought on to the project until late September, when the digging had come to a standstill. They had reached an incredibly dense rock formation that geologists called Manhattan schist. To the crew, however, the dark bedrock was better known as black devil.

After failing to break through it with traditional tools and equipment, Marek approached me with an idea. He knew that I'd studied the chemistry of explosives and wondered if I could make one strong enough to "bring the devil to his knees."

It was my proudest moment.

I was the baby of the family, always the youngest and the weakest. And now, in their greatest moment of need, my brothers and cousins had turned to me. This filled me with confidence like I had never known. Confidence that blinded me to some dangers.

I'll never forget my sense of triumph as I walked into the tunnel for the first time. There was little trace of the limp that had dogged me since my accident. I kept the serious face of a scholar as I inspected the rock formation and made detailed notes and schematics. I was determined to be impressive.

"Can you do it?" asked Marek as I reviewed my notes.

"I think so," I told him.

He stared deep into my eyes. "Think is not enough, brother. Can you do it?"

For the first time in my life, I did not back down from him. "I'm certain of it."

It was a turning point in our relationship. Although Marek was still the foreman, in many ways I took charge of the project. I was testing different combinations of black powders and South American nitrates, and he simply could not tell me how to do something he knew nothing about.

At first, I was very cautious. I experimented with small controlled blasts and then slowly added to their strength. I was happy with the results, but I was not moving fast enough for Marek. He was under great pressure from our grandfather. If our tunnel did not reach a certain length by the end of November, our contract would be given to a different company.

I told Marek that he needed to trust me. "We're close to breaking through," I assured him.

Over the course of a few weeks, however, the looks of pride I got from the rest of the crew started to disappear. So too did their confidence.

On the morning of October 31, 1896, Marek told me I was through. "It's time for you to go back to school, where you belong," he said with no emotion. "Your books and equations have no use to us out here in the real world."

I was devastated.

I couldn't bear the thought of his rejection. I couldn't face the image of walking out of that tunnel, past my family members, as a failure.

"Give me one more chance," I pleaded. "These tests have all been leading to one grand explosion. One breakthrough."

"And are we at that point?" he asked.

"We are very close."

He studied my face before saying, "You have until the end of this shift to get us there."

I was telling the truth when I said the tests had been leading to a single grand explosion, but I thought we needed at least another week to get the mixture right. His declaration meant I had ten hours to complete a week's worth of work.

At my direction, everybody started to drill small holes into the face of the rock in a specific pattern I had designed. I carefully filled the holes with all the explosive powder I had. I worked as fast as I possibly could, knowing Marek would not give me any extra time.

With fifteen minutes to go, the fuse was ready.

"Just one more set of calculations," I said as I reviewed my notes and checked them against the arrangement of explosives.

We had hurried so much in those last hours, and I wanted to make sure I hadn't overlooked anything.

"No more calculations," he said. "Is it ready or not?"

Marek only believed in definitive answers. I could not think, I had to know.

"Yes. It's ready."

We all moved into position, and Marek lit the fuse. It was then, after the fuse had been lit, but before the flame reached the explosives, that I realized my mistake. I was so focused on making the explosion strong enough to break through the rock that I hadn't fully considered that the force of a blast that big would need a place to go. Undoubtedly, it would follow the path of the tunnel right back to us.

"Oh no!" I gasped. "What have I done?"

Marek heard me, and our eyes locked. He knew what was coming, and in his face I saw anger and fury like I had never seen.

He went to say something but never got the chance.

The explosion ripped right through the bedrock and shattered it into countless tiny pieces. I had been correct. The mixture was finally strong enough to break through the schist. But the force of that explosion rocketed back toward us. It flung our bodies into the air and slammed them against the hard rock walls. Within seconds, the thirteen of us were *littered across the tunnel floor, buried under rock and dirt.*

I was dead.

My brothers and cousins were dead.

But, as I learned that day, death, especially sudden death, is not always permanent. My body had no feeling, and there was no oxygen in my lungs, but something still fired in the neurons of my brain. A single thought repeated over and over, like an old phonograph when its needle reached the end of a record.

In my mind, I was a boy back in the infirmary. I could hear my brother repeating the same phrase again and again.

"Blackwells are strong. Blackwells survive. Blackwells are strong. Blackwells survive."

And then the most unexpected thing happened. My fingers began to move.

3

Strangers on a Train

I scanned the faces in the subway station, looking to see if my mother had followed me underground. I'd spotted her two more times on our way to the Procession of the Ghouls, and even though each was just for a moment, I had the strangest sense that she was *letting* me see her. It was like she was trying to send me a message that I didn't understand. Still, I knew she'd be harder to pick out down here, where crowds of people pushed in every direction and the subway lighting played tricks on my eyes.

It also didn't help that the station was filled with the oddest assortment of people I'd ever seen. Halloween on the subway is already pretty weird, but, when the Procession of the Ghouls ends and all of those ghouls have to catch a train for home, Halloween at the Cathedral Parkway station becomes the Super Bowl of Strange.

As Grayson and I waited for the 1 train to arrive, we stood surrounded by people wearing the most elaborately grotesque costumes imaginable. Each devil or demon was spookier than the last. But none was quite as spooky as the man standing on the platform directly across from me.

At first, I thought he was dressed as an undertaker. But, when I noticed that he was doing some sort of card trick, I realized he was supposed to be a magician. (I'm guessing a good stage name for him would be Creep-O the Amazing.) He looked like he hadn't showered in months, and the rare patches of skin that weren't covered in dirt and grime were so pale you could practically see through them.

The spookiest part, though, was the card trick.

He just stared blankly into the distance as he kept flicking his right hand, making the queen of diamonds appear and disappear over and over again. The fact that he was really good at the trick made it that much creepier.

"All right, Mr. Costume Connoisseur," I whispered to Grayson. "What do you make of him? He's dressed like an undertaker, but he's doing a magic trick."

Grayson thought about it for a moment and smiled. "Maybe he's a . . . magician mortician."

"That's catchy," I said. "The Magician Mortician: He makes dead bodies disappear."

Even though we both laughed, there's no way the magician mortician could have possibly heard us or known what we were talking about. The station was way too loud. Despite this, he instantly stopped doing the trick and looked right at me with that same blank stare. He held the look and slowly began to smile until he had a big Cheshire cat grin that gave me chills. Then he started to do the trick again.

Grayson tried to lighten the mood by playing off his superhero costume. "Don't worry about him. Chemistry Man will protect you!"

"Chemistry Man?" I said with a chuckle. "*That's* your superhero name?"

"You laugh, but only Chemistry Man has . . . the equation for justice."

"Is that so?" I asked. "Well, what scientific superpower would Chemistry Man use on him?"

Grayson studied Creep-O for a moment before answering, "I'm thinking a mixture of sodium . . . potassium . . . and salts of fatty acids."

"What does that make?" I asked. "Some type of explosive?"

"No," he answered. "That makes . . . soap."

We both laughed again, but before the psycho magician could give me another death stare, the train arrived on the track between us and blocked his view. Grayson and I squeezed our way into an overstuffed car, and I breathed a sigh of relief knowing Creep-O the Amazing was waiting for a train headed in the opposite direction.

We found a space to stand at the back of the car, and as the train rattled down the tracks, I stared out the rear window into the black darkness of Dead City. My mind raced back and forth through the events of the night. I thought about the man on the news who had died handcuffed to his subway seat, and I thought about the creepy magician giving me his death stare. But mostly I thought about my mother.

"Are you okay?" asked Grayson.

I nodded and answered with a faint but convincing "Yeah."

"Really?" he said, not letting it go. "Because you don't seem okay."

(Okay, maybe it wasn't as convincing as I thought.)

"I'm just creeped out by the way that guy looked at me," I explained. "That's all."

Grayson thought for a moment, and I could tell that he wasn't sure if he should continue to push or just let it go. He decided to push.

"No, that's not all," he continued. "I'm worried about you. We're all worried about you. You haven't been yourself ever since you fought Marek on the bridge. And that makes total sense. I'm sure it was the worst thing ever. But we don't know how to help you, because you haven't really told us much about what happened up there."

I wouldn't know where to begin, I thought.

He waited for a moment to give me a chance to talk, but I just looked at him and tried to force a smile.

"I understand if you're not ready to talk about it yet," he said, softening. "But when you are, know that I'll be ready to listen."

"That means a lot," I told him. "Believe me, you'll be the first one I tell. But I'm not ready yet."

He nodded and smiled. "Okay."

We kept the conversation light until we reached Times Square, where we both had to switch trains. Even though I was headed home to Queens and he was going to Brooklyn, Grayson walked with me toward my platform.

"If you want, I can ride back with you and keep you company," he offered. "After all, I am Chemistry Man."

"Thanks, but I really am fine," I answered with a laugh. "I'll see you at school."

He flashed a heroic pose and said, "Then I'm off to fight evildoings wherever they may be." He spun around dramatically, making his cape flutter, and then he disappeared into the crowd.

I know a lot of people don't know what to make of Grayson, but I think he's awesome and hilarious. And, despite his geeky persona, he has an odd ability to be reassuring and protective. In fact, a few minutes later I wished that I hadn't been so quick to turn down his offer of company. That's because when I reached the platform for the subway to Queens, I noticed that Creep-O the Amazing was waiting for the same train.

He was talking to a woman dressed in a black leather outfit like a magician's assistant. I began to wonder if he really could do magic because I couldn't figure out how he'd gotten here so fast when he'd been waiting for a train headed in the other direction. They were standing toward the front of the platform, where the first car of the train would stop, so I hung back and waited. When the train arrived I slipped into the back of the car.

I was so focused on trying to keep track of the magician that I didn't notice the woman who sat down next to me.

"How's your hand?" she asked softly.

I looked up and saw that it was my mother. I was speechless. For years, I had imagined what it would be like to talk to her. I'd thought of a million things I wanted to say. But now, through some impossible twist of fate, she was actually talking to me, and I couldn't come up with one.

I was beyond mad and sat silently for a moment before blurting out, "What are you doing here?"

"I had to see if you were all right."

"Well, three bones in my hand are broken," I said, my voice rising. "Oh, and my dead mother's not dead. So no, I'm not all right."

She checked to make sure we weren't attracting any attention and warned, "You need to keep it quiet. If any undead see us together, you'll be in danger."

I gave her a disbelieving look and held up my cast. "In case you hadn't noticed, I already am in danger. I . . . I . . ." I was too angry to form a complete sentence.

"Molly, I know you're upset. . . ."

"Upset? You don't know anything about how I feel," I said, trying to keep my emotions together. "I was at your funeral. I listened to Dad cry himself to sleep. And it was all a lie. You're still alive." I shook my head.

"I don't know how to describe what this is," she said. "But it's not *alive*."

When we reached the next station, she stopped talking and checked out the faces of everyone who got on or off our car. I waited until the train started back up and we reentered the darkness of the subway tunnel before asking, "If it's not alive, then what is it?"

"It's a way to look out for you."

"*You* look out for *me*?" I asked, still disbelieving.

"Yes," she said. "To make sure you're safe."

"If you're so concerned with my safety, then why did you leave me at the top of the George Washington Bridge? I was injured. You know how scared I am of heights. Oh, and I'd just come face-to-face with the mother who'd died two and a half years earlier."

"I wanted to stay, but it was too far from the Manhattan schist," she explained. "I could already feel my body changing. I couldn't have lasted any longer without degenerating into a Level 3. As it was, it's taken me this long just to regain my strength."

Actually, this thought had occurred to me. While we were on the bridge, I'd noticed her weakening. I paused for a moment and asked, "Then when do you look out for me?"

"I watch you go to school. Some days, like today, I fol-

low you when you leave the campus and stay in Manhattan. Just like sometimes I hang out near your dad's fire station so I can see him for a second or two."

I was trying to stay calm, but inside I was freaking out. It was all more than I could handle, and it only got worse once we pulled into the Fifth Avenue station. Over the loudspeaker, the conductor announced that our next stop was Lexington Avenue, which is the last one before the train leaves Manhattan. My mom would have to get off there, or she'd wind up like the guy they'd found on the train that morning in Brooklyn. I could tell that she was thinking the same thing, because she started talking faster.

"How's Beth?" she asked. "I see you at school, and I see Dad at the station. But I don't have any way to know when she's coming in from Queens. I haven't seen her since I was sick at the hospital. How's she doing?"

"Well, she thinks her mother's dead," I said coldly.

Mom sagged, and for the first time in the conversation I felt something other than anger and confusion. I felt bad for her. "She's doing well," I offered. "Really well."

She smiled. "Are you guys getting along?"

I laughed and asked, "Do you want me to tell you the truth or what I think you want to hear?"

Before she could answer, I saw the magician mortician

again. He had made his way back through the train, going from car to car, and now he was in ours. At first, I thought he was looking for me, but then I realized that he was performing magic tricks for the passengers while his assistant held out the top hat for people to give them money. The tricks were actually very good, but the creepy factor and his lack of showering made it so that few people made donations.

"Can you focus for a second?" Mom asked. "Lexington Avenue is next, and that's where I have to get off."

"I can get off with you," I offered hopefully. "We can talk about everything."

She shook her head. "I'd love nothing more, but it wouldn't be safe for you. Just tell me something about you, your father, Beth. Tell me anything."

It's amazing how when you have to think of something on the spot, your mind is a total blank. It took me a moment to come up with any news about the family. "Beth made varsity cheerleading and is thinking about going to NYU. Dad's still dopey as ever. He made lasagna for my birthday; it was delicious. And I'm an Omega. But I guess you already knew that."

She smiled proudly. "Molly, you're not just an Omega," she said. "You're amazing. . . ."

It was right then, just as my mother was about to compliment me on my Omega awesomeness, when I began to realize something was wrong. The magician had now reached our end of the car and stood only a few feet away from us as he did a trick with a pair of handcuffs.

His assistant cuffed him behind his back and then covered them with a black handkerchief. Somehow he managed to slip out of them and escape. It was impressive, and this time a few of the passengers clapped and even tossed money into the hat.

That's when I remembered the news story about the zombie whose body had been discovered that morning. The victim had been handcuffed to the subway seat.

I was still putting it together as we pulled into the Lexington Avenue station and the magician smiled right at me. Unlike earlier, this time he showed his teeth, which were bright yellow and orange. Before I could even react, he'd used his magician's sleight of hand to slip one of the handcuffs around my mother's wrist. . . .

Ω4

I Reconnect with Mom

The magician's plan was simple. He had one handcuff around my mother's wrist and was trying to lock the other onto the frame of her seat. If he succeeded, there was no saving her. She would be trapped on the train, unable to get off before it left Manhattan. Considering she'd already died on me once, I was not about to let it happen again.

My first move was to club him across the face with my cast. I'd accidentally hit myself with it enough times to know it could cause some damage, but I was pleasantly surprised when it completely dislocated his nose. It also dazed him long enough for me to shove him away and break his grip on the handcuffs and my mother.

Just then, the train stopped, the sliding doors opened, and both the magician and his assistant escaped into the Lexington Avenue station, hoping to blend into the crowd. Apparently, they were unaware that freakishly tall, unwashed zombies dressed in magician/mortician costumes do not blend in. Anywhere. Even on Halloween.

My mom and I jumped up and started to follow, but when she stepped onto the platform, she turned around and held up her hand for me to stop. "Stay on the train and get home safely," she said. "I'll take care of this."

There we were, just inches away but worlds apart, my feet on the subway, hers on the platform. I wanted to say something, but I couldn't find the words.

"But there's one thing you need to know," she continued. "Something I should have told you on the bridge."

"What?"

She looked at me with the mom look I'd missed so much and said, "You need to know that I love you, Molly. You need to know that you're my hero."

Okay, technically that was *two* things. But, considering they were the two nicest things anyone has ever said to me, I ignored the mistake.

I also ignored her instructions.

We may have some pretty big issues to work out, but there was no way I was going to let the doors close with us on opposite sides. I slipped through just as they were sliding shut.

"Okay," I said, pumped and ready to go. "Let's go get 'em."

Considering we were in the middle of a chase with two killer zombies, I assumed she would jump into action. Like right at that very moment. But, of course, I forgot who I was dealing with, because my mom decided *this* was the perfect time for a lecture on listening.

"Didn't I tell you to stay on the train?" she asked. "I couldn't have been any clearer. I said, 'Stay on the train and get home safely.' It's just like your birthday party at the Central Park Zoo."

I slumped in total disbelief.

"Can we not do this?" I asked. "Can we please not relive the Central Park Zoo story . . . again? I'm sorry you were so worried, but I was *five years old*. Five-year-olds make mistakes."

"And, apparently, they never learn from them," she said. "Because you still don't listen to a word I say."

It was the same old Mom, like we'd ridden some sort

of subway time machine back to one her countless "teachable moments." And just like she always did, she used her hands a lot when she was trying to make a point. Except now she had a pair of handcuffs attached to one of those hands, and when she gestured, they bounced around in every direction.

"You might want to hide those," I said as I motioned toward a transit cop standing just a few feet away. "They'd be pretty hard to explain."

She nodded and quickly jammed her hand and the cuffs into her coat pocket. Since I really wasn't in the mood to continue the lecture, I just started following the zombies again, and she had no choice but to do the same.

The two of them were headed for the far end of the platform, where they could make a run for the open tunnel and vanish into Dead City. Mom's mini lecture had given them a pretty good head start, but we caught a break when another transit cop stepped out from behind a column in the middle of the platform. There was no way they could get down onto the tracks and into the tunnel with him standing there. He would have arrested them on the spot.

They turned back and saw us coming right at them. Unless one of Creep-O the Amazing's tricks was literally making people disappear, we were about to have them cornered. Out of desperation, they hurried through a maintenance door marked AUTHORIZED PERSONNEL ONLY.

It looked like the door to a storage closet, and when we got there, I was sure we had them trapped. Mom, however, was still in lecture mode. I went to open the door, but she slapped her palm against it and held it shut.

"We still haven't settled the part about you not staying on the train."

"Yeah," I said, nodding. "In fact, there are a lot of things we still haven't settled. But I don't think we have the time to go through them all right now. So unless you really want to stand here and argue, I say we take care of the two zombies who just tried to kill you."

She considered this for a second and gave me a faint smile. "I go first."

"Just be ready for whatever's on the other side of that door," I replied with confidence. "I already had to save you on the train. Don't make me do it again."

"Is that so?" she asked, giving the attitude right back at me. "And who saved who on the bridge?"

"Who saved *whom*," I said, correcting her like she always used to do to me. "Just because we're in the middle of a crisis doesn't mean it's okay to use bad grammar."

We both laughed. Now we were a team. We'd gone from mother and daughter to Omega and Omega. Okay, one was undead and retired and the other suspended, but after all, the saying is *Omega today, Omega forever.*

She checked to make sure neither transit cop was looking our way, and then she opened the door. I think we both expected to find two angry zombies crammed into a storage closet.

We were wrong.

It turns out that the Lexington Avenue station was originally built to be twice its current size. This door opened up onto the other half, which was now an abandoned ghost station, complete with dust-covered platforms and empty tunnels. Instead of a closet, the magician and his assistant had found the perfect escape route.

"It would not be good if they made it back to tell their friends about us," my mother said as we ran after them.

"I don't plan on letting them get away," I replied, turning up the speed.

The two of them were about twenty yards ahead of us, but they'd made a huge mistake. They'd already gotten down onto the track bed, and the gravel made it difficult to run. We stayed up on the platform, where the only thing blocking us was the occasional spiderweb. (Although at one point I did get some web in my mouth, which was beyond gross.)

It took me about two-thirds of the platform to catch up with them. When I did, I jumped off the platform and crashed right on top of Creep-O the Amazing. A few seconds later, I heard Mom tackle his partner.

We rolled around on the gravel for a moment before we were able to get back on our feet. I squared off against him, and my confidence got a huge boost when I saw how badly I'd dislocated his nose with the punch on the train. It was all twisted and turned to the side.

"Wow," I said as I tried to get him worked up. "It's the first time I've ever seen someone who can actually smell his own eye."

"Really?" my mother said as she lined up against his leather-clad assistant. "All those years of Jeet Kune Do and your plan of attack is to taunt him?"

(Is there some rule that says moms can never let you seem cool? Even for a second?)

"Are you going to criticize everything I do?" I asked.

"Nope," she responded as she flashed a smile at me. "Just the things you do wrong."

Both of us turned to face our opponents and unleashed a flurry of attack moves. I'll be honest and admit I was trying to show off a little. I wanted Mom to know I had major skills. But the fight was much harder than I expected. First of all, I'm left-handed, but my left hand was in a cast, so I had to fight the opposite way I normally do. Second, it turns out that the sleight of hand and deception skills magicians use to pull off their tricks also make them difficult to fight.

I kept thinking he was going one way when he was actually going the other. At one point, he even distracted me with that stupid card trick he'd been doing earlier on the train platform. While my attention was momentarily focused on the card as it disappeared and reappeared, he knocked me down with a leg swipe.

I came back at him strong and really thought I had it won when I yanked his arm completely off his body. It was the same thing I'd done to the first zombie I ever fought. Except it turned out that it wasn't a real arm. It was a fake one he used for one of his tricks. Ugh. (So much for demonstrating my impressive skills.)

As I stared in disbelief at what I was holding, he leveled me with a punch that slammed me against the ground. I looked up and wiped the gravel from my face just in time to see my mother whip the handcuffs around her wrists like a weapon and whack him right in the face. She followed it up with a couple of lightning-quick punches that reminded me of her reputation as the ultimate Zeke, which stands for ZK or "zombie killer."

"You still keeping track of who's saving *whom*?" she said, exaggerating the word.

"I am if you are," I answered as I leapt up and saved her right back by cutting off the assistant who was just about to jump her from behind. It was surreal to fight a pair of zombies side by side with my mother. I guess this was our version of playing catch in the backyard. But so much more fun.

At least, it *was* more fun, until the moment where I reared back to throw a punch at the assistant, only to have Creep-O grab my arm from behind. Before I realized what was happening, he'd slapped the other handcuff around my wrist.

Now my mother and I were literally connected to each other like a pair of prisoners. We wound up back to back, trying to fight them with one hand each. And this was when she decided to take another trip down memory lane.

"You remember swing dancing?" she asked.

I couldn't believe she was choosing this moment to revisit another one of our failures. When I was nine, she signed us up for mother-daughter swing dancing classes. It was something she and my sister Beth had done the previous year. They'd loved it and thought it brought them closer together. She wanted to have the same experience with me, except unlike my sister I have no rhythm. I was terrible at it and quickly grew to despise everything about it. I began coming up with all sorts of lame excuses to miss, and eventually, Mom got the hint. It was a sore subject for a while and not something I wanted to reminisce about in the current situation.

"First the Central Park Zoo and now swing dancing," I said. "Are we going to go through every mistake I've ever made?"

"That's not what I meant," she said. "I just wanted to know if you remember the Big Finish."

The Big Finish was what our teacher called the finale of the dance we learned. For the move, we had to stand back to back and lock our arms together. Then Mom leaned forward and flipped me over her head so that I landed face-to-face with her. It was the only thing from swing dancing that I enjoyed.

It was also something we could do even if we were handcuffed together.

"Got it," I said as I locked my arms into hers. "On three."

"One . . . two . . . three," she counted off.

She snapped forward, and I started to flip over her. On the way up, I did a scissors kick and nailed the magician's assistant right under the chin with my foot. On the way back down, I popped Creep-O with a head shot that laid him out.

It took a moment to realize what had just happened. My mother looked at the two of them in amazement. "Unbelievable! You managed to kill two zombies in a single move."

I smiled broadly. "I guess that's why they call it the Big Finish."

We both laughed and tried an awkward high five. (Awkward because we were handcuffed and because of my whole lack of rhythm thing.)

She unlocked the cuffs with a key she dug out of the magician's coat pocket, and we snuck back into the subway station to wait for my train. Whatever issues we'd had before were now, at least for the moment, overshadowed by what we'd just been through.

According to the electronic sign on the wall, the next train was four minutes away. That didn't leave a lot of time for catching up.

"So, is your plan to keep following me around?" I asked.

She nodded. "Pretty much."

"What if I need to get in contact with you? Is there some sort of phone number I can call or a Bat-signal I can flash?"

"No, but you're right. . . . We do need a way for you to reach me." She thought for a moment and smiled. "Your birthday at the Central Park Zoo."

"Again with the zoo story?" I couldn't believe it.

"Relax," she said. "Remember when you got lost, where did I find you?"

"Watching the big clock with the dancing animals."

"Right," she said. "And if you need me, that's where I'll find you again."

"You want me to stand there and wait under the clock?"

"No, just leave a coded message there," she said. "I'll check it every day."

"It's not exactly e-mail," I said. "But I like it."

We stood there, unsure what to say, our conversation frozen by awkwardness. Finally, I spoke up. "They told me you were the greatest Zeke of all time, and now I can see why. You were amazing."

"Me? You killed two zombies with one move. You're the star, Molly. I have no doubt that you'll be the best Omega ever."

"Don't be so sure," I said.

I explained about our team getting suspended and the

review hearing scheduled for the next week. She thought about this for a moment.

"If you think they're going to rule against you," she said, "tell them that you have to be reinstated to work on the Baker's Dozen."

"What's the Baker's Dozen?" I asked.

"It's a long-running top secret assignment," she replied. "It supersedes the review panel and the Prime Omega. They have to reinstate you if you get asked to join it by one of the teams that are already part of it."

"What if they figure out that no one really asked us?"

She smiled. "But I just did."

Suddenly, a thought occurred to me. "Are you still part of an Omega team?"

"Maybe," she said with a sly smile.

Then we heard the train approaching the station, and she quickly explained exactly what I needed to say during the review hearing. The train came to a stop, and it was time for me to get on. She gave me a hug, and I melted. I couldn't stay mad at her.

I stepped on and turned back to tell her one last thing.

"I'll figure out a way for you to see Beth. I promise."

The doors closed, and she mouthed the words *thank you* and pressed her hand against her heart.

Ω 5

Triskaidekaphobia

The massive steps in front of the Museum of Natural History were overrun with different groups ready to go inside. The loudest was the mob of elementary students piling off a row of school buses from the Bronx, and the most colorful was the cluster of kids, parents, and grandparents wearing bright pink sweatshirts marked BERGER FAMILY REUNION. But the smallest, and by far the most anxious, was the collection of four people standing at the base of the giant statue of Teddy Roosevelt astride his horse.

It was my Omega team.

Unlike the other groups, we hadn't come to explore the dinosaur exhibits or stare in amazement at the giant blue whale hanging from the ceiling of the Hall of Ocean Life. We'd come for our review hearing, and Natalie wanted to give us some last-minute coaching before we headed inside.

"According to Dr. H, a review panel has never overturned a ruling of the Prime Omega," she said. "But that doesn't mean there can't be a first time. We just need to admit our mistakes, assure them that they won't happen again, and convince everybody that we're worthy of a second chance."

Alex and Grayson both nodded in agreement.

"Actually," I said, "I've got another idea."

Natalie wasn't exactly looking for opposing viewpoints, so she was a bit perturbed as she asked, "What's that?"

I wanted to tell them about the Baker's Dozen. My mom had assured me that it would save our team. But I didn't know how to do it without telling them everything, and I wasn't ready for that. Still, there was no escaping the fact that I had created this problem. That meant I should to be the one to fix it. I'd been mulling it over for days and had come up with only one solution.

"Why don't we tell them the truth?" I suggested. "Tell them that everything was my fault and that you were just trying to protect me. Then they can kick me out of Omega, and you guys can find someone to replace me on the team. That was Dr. H's original verdict, so they can accept it without overruling him."

Alex reached over and put his hand on my shoulder. "You just don't get it, Molly. We're not interested in being a team without you."

"That's right," Grayson added. "We're a package deal. Either they want us all, or they don't want any of us. Got it?"

I looked at Natalie to make sure she agreed. Then I nodded and said, "Got it."

"Good," she replied. "Now, let's go do this."

We went inside and took the elevator to the fourth floor. According to our instructions, we were supposed to wait by the skeleton of the Tyrannosaurus rex. Someone was going to meet us there and take us to the hearing.

Even though I was nervous about everything, just being in the dinosaur hall made me smile. It was one of my favorite places on earth.

"This is where it all started," I said, looking up at the dinosaur's massive jaw.

"What do you mean?" asked Grayson.

"I was five years old, and my dad put me up on his shoulders so I could get a closer look at T. rex here." I closed my eyes as I pictured the memory in my head. "It was love at first sight."

Grayson laughed. "You fell in love with a massive theropod with tiny arms whose name means 'tyrant lizard king'?"

"Head over heels," I said as I looked around the room at all the other dinosaurs. "I fell in love with all of them. That was the day I fell in love with science."

"Well," said Alex, "let's hope our Omega team doesn't join your boyfriend on the extinction list."

"Yes, let's hope," said a voice from behind us.

We turned and saw that it was Dr. Hidalgo. Dr. H was my mom's best friend and colleague at the coroner's office. They'd been a part of the same Omega team when they were in school and he'd become the Prime Omega— or Prime-O—in charge of all the Omega teams. He'd had to step down from that position because we'd been forced to uncover his identity.

As usual, Dr. H was sharply dressed in a perfectly pressed dress shirt and pants and wore a stylish bow tie. He also wore a friendly smile, which was a big departure from the last time we'd seen him. (That would be the day he suspended our team for breaking countless rules and procedures.)

Smile or not, I wasn't sure how he was feeling toward us, and me in particular. I offered a rather faint "Hello, Dr. Hidalgo" and tried to avoid eye contact.

He wasn't having any of that. He placed a firm finger under my chin and lifted it until I was looking him right in the eye. "Molly Bigelow, how long have I known you?"

"My whole life," I said weakly.

"Then act like it."

He held his arms out, and I gave him a hug.

"No matter what happened before and no matter what the panel decides today, nothing changes what you mean to me." He gave me one last squeeze and then turned to the others. "Now follow me."

Dr. Hidalgo had been a family friend for as long as I could remember. One of the things that I had been dreading most about this day was the thought that we were opposing each other. Talking to him now made me feel a whole lot better about everything.

He led us beyond the exhibits, down a maze of hallways, and past a couple of security checkpoints. At each one, he just flashed a badge and the guards waved us through with no questions asked. Finally, we stepped into a giant freight elevator.

"It's big," Grayson said, referring to the size.

"Big enough to hold a dinosaur," Dr. H pointed out as he pressed the button for the basement.

"If we're going to the basement, why did you have us meet you on the fourth floor?" asked Grayson.

He looked back at me over his shoulder and then turned to face the others. "Because it's Molly's favorite place, and I thought it might help calm her nerves."

Natalie gave me a sideways glance and a smile. This was the Dr. H we both knew.

As we rode in the elevator, he gave us a rundown of what to expect.

"It's pretty straightforward," he explained. "I'll go first and tell them why I suspended you. Then you'll make a statement and answer any questions from the review panel."

From the elevator, we went down another hallway until we reached a large lecture hall. The room was built like an auditorium, with steep banks of seating that looked down on the stage.

"This is a sacred room," Dr. H told us. "More than a century ago, this is where the museum's paleontologists presented their initial findings about dinosaurs and prehistoric life. Ever since, this is where some of the true legends of scientific thought have shared their discoveries."

"And this is where our hearing is taking place?" Natalie asked.

"Yes."

"How did we get such an important room?" asked Grayson.

Dr. H smiled. "Let's just say that some of the legends of scientific thought also happen to be Omegas, too."

"Cool," Grayson said, echoing what we were all thinking. "Very cool."

In the middle of the stage were four wooden chairs. Dr. H motioned for us to sit in them, and we each took our place. The lighting was so bright that we couldn't really see what was happening out in the auditorium. If I squinted, I could make out some shapes and shadows but no faces. The identities of the past Omegas had to be kept secret, even from us.

It all happened just like Dr. Hidalgo told us it would in the elevator. He went first and talked about the team and our past accomplishments. He also pointed out that I was the daughter of Rosemary Collins, whom he called "my dearest friend and a legendary Omega." Then he gave a detailed report of all the mistakes we'd made. This included my unauthorized visit to Dead City, when I crashed the flatline party and had to escape underwater in the Old

Croton Aqueduct, as well as our team's trip underground to see Marek Blackwell.

Next, Natalie spoke on behalf of the team, and she was amazing. She talked about successful assignments they'd completed before I was part of the team and how they went about selecting me to join them. She sang all of our praises and went into detail about how I had kept the *Book of Secrets* from falling into the hands of the undead. By the time she was done, I knew they were going to reverse the suspension.

I was wrong.

The questions were relentless. "Why did you go into Dead City when you knew it was against the rules?" The fact that we couldn't see the people asking the questions was disorienting. "Why didn't you alert the Prime-O the moment you found the photographs of the Unlucky 13 along with the *Book of Secrets*?" Voices came from every direction. "What exactly happened with you, Miss Bigelow, and Marek atop the George Washington Bridge?"

After about fifteen minutes, it was obvious things were not going well. My teammates looked defeated, and I had to do something. I leaned toward them.

"I can save us, but you can't ask me how I know," I whispered.

Natalie had a confused look on her face. "What?"

"I know a way to save us," I said a bit louder. "But if I do it, you can't ask me how I know. You just have to accept it."

She shook her head. "If we're a team, we have to trust one another."

"I do trust you," I replied. "But you have to trust me that if I say I can't tell, it's for a good reason."

She thought for a second and nodded. "Just do it."

I looked at the others, and they nodded too.

"Excuse me," an annoyed voice called down to us. "I hate to interrupt your conversation, but we need you to answer our questions."

I looked at the others one more time to make sure, and then I turned toward the unseen woman.

"I apologize," I said. "Can you please repeat your last question?"

"Is there any other reason you can give us that would make us reconsider your suspension?"

"Yes, there is," I said, taking a deep breath. "Our team needs to be reinstated because we've been asked to work on the Baker's Dozen."

Suddenly, things on the other side of the lights got very quiet. My teammates looked at me, wondering what on earth I was talking about. Dr. H considered this for a moment and begrudgingly smiled.

Now a different voice called down to us. It was one we hadn't heard before, a pleasant voice belonging to a man who sounded older than the others.

"Could you please repeat that?" he asked.

"I said we have to be reinstated because we've been asked to help on the Baker's Dozen."

"That's what I thought you said," he replied before pausing and adding, "I'll have to ask everyone except for the Prime-O to leave the room."

Natalie, Alex, Grayson, and I all stood up to exit, but the man chuckled and called down to us again. "You four stay. I was talking to everyone else."

"Good luck," Dr. H said with a wink as he got up and left.

Now my teammates really gave me confused looks, and all I could do was shrug. My mom had told me what to say, but I had no idea what it all meant. We heard the others collect their things and leave, and soon the only noise was the sound of the lights humming. Then the older man had a brief conversation with the woman who had asked the last question. (I guess that means she's the new Prime-O.)

"What's the current status of the Baker's Dozen?" he asked her.

"We're down to two teams," she said. "One current and one made up of past Omegas."

It occurred to me that my mother must be part of the second team, a fact that made me smile.

"I thought we added a new team last month," he said, a bit bewildered.

"We tried, sir," she said, "but they were unable to solve the riddle."

He thought about that for a moment. "Well, then I guess they wouldn't have done too well on this assignment. Were you aware that a new invitation had been given out?"

"No, sir," she said, "but they don't need approval from me to extend one."

Now the man directed his attention toward us. "Molly, can you confirm that you truly have been asked to help on the Baker's Dozen?"

I repeated the response exactly as my mother had told me on the subway platform. "I can confirm that Triskaidekaphobia is the irrational fear of the number thirteen."

"And do you suffer from this phobia?" he asked.

"No," I answered, staying to the script. "Because, like the number thirteen, I am completely rational."

"That's very good to hear," he replied.

We all waited for a moment to see if there was more.

"Does that mean we're reinstated?" asked Natalie.

"Yes," he said to our relief before adding, "with one catch."

We traded nervous looks and then turned our attention back to him.

"What's that?" I asked.

"The Baker's Dozen is a top-secret operation," he explained. "In fact, it's so secretive that we cannot discuss it here."

"Then how do we find out about it?" asked Natalie.

"By solving a puzzle," he said. "If you can figure out this riddle, it will lead you to everything you need to know about the Baker's Dozen."

"And if we can't?" I asked nervously.

"Well, then you're back where you started," he answered. "How do you think the hearing was going?"

"Not well," I answered, stating the obvious.

"No, it wasn't," he said. "So I suggest you solve it."

"What's the riddle?"

"With this iron, you cannot press a shirt, but you can press your luck."

Ω6

Pressing Our Luck

Since Natalie's apartment is only six blocks from the museum, we decided to go there to try solving the riddle. Alex was especially pleased with this decision when he found out that there was still plenty of leftover British Halloween candy. "That will definitely help," he said with a straight face. "British candy's good for thinking."

"And you base that claim on what?" Natalie asked with a raised eyebrow.

"It's a well-known fact," he answered. "How do you think Isaac Newton came up with all the laws of motion? Chocolate."

Considering we had just been reinstated, you'd think everyone would have been in a better mood as we walked along Central Park West. But there was definitely some tension, and I was pretty sure this had to do with the "You can't ask me any questions" requirement I put on saving the team. To their credit, they didn't ask. But they also didn't say much of anything else.

Part of me wanted to blurt it all out and tell them about my mom and what happened on the bridge and the fight with the magician and his assistant. They had proven their friendship and trust to me more times than I could count. But Mom told me it would be dangerous if anyone knew about her. And I kind of worried what they'd think of me if they knew my mother was a zombie. Would they begin to question my loyalty to Omega? I mulled this over for a couple blocks as the cold November wind turned my cheeks a nice bright shade of pink. Finally, I decided to tell them the truth.

Well, sort of.

I told them about my mother approaching me on the subway and telling me what to say about the Baker's Dozen. Only I left out the part about her being my mother. I just said it was a past Omega who wanted our team to work on the project. Technically, it was all true. But I'd left out some important facts.

I think Natalie was about to push for some more details, but Grayson saved me by changing the subject. "Do you think it's significant that 'baker's dozen' and 'triskaideka-phobia' both have something to do with the number thir-teen?" he asked.

I thought about this for a second and realized I had no idea what he was talking about. "What does 'baker's dozen' have to do with the number thirteen? Aren't there twelve in a dozen?"

"Usually," he said. "But in the Middle Ages, there were strict laws against bakers overcharging. If an order of bread was underweight, the baker could get his hand chopped off as a penalty. So they'd add an extra piece to every order to make sure there was enough."

"Which means if you ordered twelve," I said, under-standing, "you'd get thirteen."

"A baker's dozen."

Only Grayson would be familiar with medieval baking laws. I was truly impressed. "Is there anything you don't know?"

He thought about it for a moment. "Well, I don't know the answer to the riddle."

We all laughed, which finally broke the tension.

For the rest of the walk, we tried to solve the riddle. We

talked about ironing clothes, dry cleaning, and anything else that might relate to an iron. We played around with the phrase "push your luck." But we got nowhere. We were totally stumped. We were also well aware of the fact that the last team that had tried to solve the riddle had failed, which was something we could not afford to do.

By the time we got to Natalie's building, the only thing we knew for sure was that the lobby was nice and warm. My face had already started to thaw as we stepped onto the elevator.

"Here's an example of triskaidekaphobia for you," Natalie said as she pushed the button for the twelfth floor. "There's no thirteen."

"Seriously?" I said.

I looked at the panel and couldn't believe my eyes. Sure enough, the button next to the twelve was fourteen.

"There's no thirteenth floor on this building? Because of a silly phobia?"

"That's true of a lot of the older buildings in New York," Grayson said. "People were so scared of living or working on the thirteenth floor, they would just skip that number. There's no thirteenth floor in the Chrysler Building or at 30 Rock."

Like I said, there was virtually nothing Grayson didn't know.

"Speaking of phobias," I said as the elevator began its climb, "I hope everyone notices that I'm going up to Natalie's apartment. Again. That's the second time this month I've overcome my fear of heights."

"Are you counting Halloween as the first time?" asked Alex.

"Yes!" I said. "Why wouldn't I?"

"I seem to remember you screaming in fear," he joked.

"At the movie . . . and it was just a flinch," I said as I gave him a slug.

"So how have you overcome this fear?" asked Grayson.

I thought about it for a moment before saying, "Once you've been in a fight on top of a bridge six hundred and fifty feet in the air, a twelfth-floor luxury apartment doesn't seem so scary anymore."

"Good point," Natalie said.

The elevator dinged and the doors opened onto Natalie's floor. But when the others started to get off, I motioned for them to stay and said, "Wait."

"She jinxed it," Alex said. "She talked about it and now she's scared of heights again."

"Wrong phobia," I replied, on the verge of a breakthrough.

"What do you mean?" asked Grayson.

I pointed at the panel of buttons. "Because of triskaidekaphobia, you can't press a button for thirteen."

"Yeah," Natalie replied. "That's kind of what we just said."

"Don't you see? It's just like the riddle," I explained. "You can't press the number thirteen. You can't *press* your luck."

"Oooh," Alex said. "That's good."

The others nodded and for the first time in a while, we felt like an actual Omega team. We went into the apartment and settled in the family room to work on the puzzle. Natalie and Grayson sat at the computer, Alex kicked back in a recliner, happily munching from the bowl of Halloween candy. And I took the chair that was farthest from the window. (I may have been getting better at dealing with heights, but there was no reason to tempt fate and sit by the massive twelfth-story picture window.)

"Let's break down the riddle piece by piece," Grayson said. "With this iron, you cannot press a shirt, but you can press your luck."

"I'm on board with Molly's elevator theory," Alex said midchew. "I'm thinking it's an elevator that has a button for the thirteenth floor."

"But what does that have to do with an iron?" asked Natalie. "And what elevator?"

He thought for a second before answering, "I have no idea."

"Wow! You were right. That chocolate really does make you as smart as Isaac Newton," she said sarcastically.

"What about an elevator made of iron?" I suggested.

"That could be," Grayson said with a nod as he typed in a search and scanned the results. "There's an elevator made out of iron in Brooklyn, but it's a grain elevator, so there wouldn't be buttons for any floor."

"What if the elevator isn't made out of iron?" Alex wondered. "What if it's the building?"

"Can you make a building out of iron?" asked Natalie. "I don't think it's strong enough."

"Maybe not," Grayson said as he looked at the results of another search. "But there are some buildings in SoHo with cast-iron facades."

"Any of them thirteen stories high?" I asked.

He shook his head. "Nope."

"I think we're getting off track," Natalie said. "The riddle said, 'With *this* iron, you cannot press a shirt.' I don't think it's talking about the metal. I think it's talking about one specific iron."

Grayson kept running through search after search on the computer. He called out to us whenever he found something potentially useful. "At the Metropolitan Museum of Art, there's a Degas painting called *A Woman Ironing*."

"Is there anything lucky or unlucky about it?" I asked.

"Other than having to do chores," he said, "not particularly."

"What about this one," Natalie said, looking farther down the same list. "There's also a painting of St. Reparata being tortured with hot irons. That sounds extremely unlucky."

"I got it!" Alex exclaimed.

We all stopped and turned eagerly to him.

"Really?" Natalie said. "You figured it out?"

"Umm . . . no," he said, guiltily holding up a candy bar. "I meant I found the specific type of chocolate bar I was looking for. It has nuts and caramel I had one on Halloween. It's really delicious."

Natalie balled up a piece of paper and threw it at him.

"Here's one at the Museum of Modern Art by the artist Man Ray," Grayson said. "It's a painted flatiron with tacks glued along the bottom."

"Does that even count as art?" Natalie asked, leaning in to get a closer look at the picture.

"Forget the art museums," Alex said. "It's not *Flatiron with Tacks*."

"Wait," I said excitedly. "That's it."

"It *is Flatiron with Tacks?*" asked Alex, confused.

"Not the tacks, just the flatiron," I said. "Look up the Flatiron Building."

Grayson smiled as he typed. A moment later, a picture of the Flatiron Building was on the computer screen. Grayson read the description next to it. "Completed in 1902, the Flatiron Building is considered a pioneering skyscraper of historical significance. The building is shaped like a triangle and gets its name from its resemblance to a similarly shaped clothes iron."

By now, Alex and I had both gotten up and were looking over Grayson's shoulder, reading along with him.

"Does it have a thirteenth floor?" Alex asked anxiously.

Grayson clicked on a couple links and found the answer. "Yes, it does!"

"Well, Molly, it's a good thing you're getting over your fear of heights," Natalie said, "because it looks like we've got an elevator to catch."

Ω 7

The Room That Isn't There

The Flatiron is the only building I know that has its own optical illusion. That's because it's a giant triangle. If you stand at just the right spot and look at the front, you can make it seem like half the building vanishes. The security guard in the lobby, however, was not an illusion. And there was no trick to make him disappear. Too bad, because we needed to get past him in order to reach the elevators.

Our plan was to quickly check the directory on the wall and see which companies had offices on the thirteenth floor. Then we could try to convince the guard that we had an appointment with one of those companies. It was a good plan . . . except for one small problem.

"There are no floor numbers," Alex said as he looked at the list, "just the names of the companies."

Ugh.

There were at least fifty companies listed on the directory, and rather than arranged by floor, they were listed alphabetically. If we'd solved the riddle correctly (and I had a good feeling that we had), one of them held the secret to the Baker's Dozen. But we had no idea which one it was. We also didn't have much time to figure it out. Our sense of desperation must have caught the guard's attention, because after a few moments, he got up from his desk and started walking toward us.

"Stall him," Natalie whispered.

"Yeah," I said in agreement. "Stall him."

She gave me a nudge. "I was talking to you."

"*Me?* How am I supposed to stall him?"

"Be creative."

You've got to love the way Natalie gives advice that has absolutely no actual advice in it. I decided the best thing to do was to start talking to the guard before he got a chance to ask us any questions. That way, at least, I could direct the conversation. So I just asked him the first thing that came to mind.

"Excuse me, but how do you know which side's the front?"

He stopped for a moment and tried to figure out what I was talking about. "I'm sorry, what?"

"Which side of the building is the front?" I asked. "Square buildings have a front, a back, and two sides. But with a triangular building, how can you tell which side is the front?"

He gave me the same look I give my Latin teacher whenever she asks me to conjugate verbs. You know, the look that says, "I should probably know this, but I have absolutely no idea." I decided to keep piling on.

"I mean, the side facing Fifth Avenue looks like the front. But so does the side facing Broadway. Does it have two fronts? Can a building even have two fronts? Is that possible? Or does it just have two sides and no front?"

"Those are all good questions," he said. And while he was busy trying to come up with an answer to any of them, the others kept searching the directory for any hint as to where we needed to go.

The stall was working perfectly until an uninvited guest jumped into the conversation. Apparently, the fact that I was not actually looking for an answer did not matter. A question had been asked, and Encyclopedia Grayson couldn't help himself.

"Fifth Avenue is the front."

He said it like a fact and not like an opinion. And, knowing Grayson, I'm certain he was right. Still, I gave him my angry eyes, hoping he'd get the hint and help out.

"Are you sure?" I asked as I pointed to a photograph of the building that was hanging on the wall. "Both sides look identical. Why isn't Broadway the front?"

"Yeah," wondered the guard. "Why not Broadway?"

"Because the address is 175 Fifth Avenue," he explained. "According to the US Postal Service, the address signifies the front of the building."

"Hey, that makes perfect sense," said the guard. "I could have thought about that all day and never figured it out."

"Yeah, thanks for clearing that up," I added, still staring daggers at Grayson. "I would have hated to waste any more of his time."

By Grayson's reaction, I could see that he finally realized his mistake.

"Sorry," he whispered.

The guard now turned to the others and asked, "So, what brings you all to the Flatiron?"

"Well," Natalie replied, taking the lead. "We have an appointment on the thirteenth floor."

"Great," he said as he moved back toward the desk. "Just come on over, and I'll sign you in."

We all breathed a sigh of relief. This might be easy after all.

"I just need to know who the appointment's with," he continued.

And then again, it might not. We stood quietly for a moment until Natalie stammered a very unconvincing, "You mean who on the thirteenth floor?"

But out of nowhere Alex stepped forward and answered, "Palindrome Games."

The guard handed us the sign-in sheet. "I should have guessed. Are you the game testers?"

Without missing a beat, Alex nodded and said, "Yes. Yes, we are. We're the game testers."

We signed in and walked straight onto the elevator. Sure enough, it had a button for the thirteenth floor.

"Ready to press your luck?" Natalie said as she pushed the gold button.

The moment the doors closed, I slugged Grayson in the arm. "Thanks a lot, Mr. United States Postal Service."

"I said I was sorry," he protested. "I can't help myself. When I know the right answer, I have to say it."

"Speaking of right answers," Natalie said, turning to

Alex. "How'd you come up with Palindrome Games?"

"It was on the directory."

"Yeah," she replied. "But so were about fifty other companies."

"True," Alex said. "But none with 'Omega' hidden in the middle of their names."

Sure enough, the last three letters of "Palindrome" and the first two of "Games" spell "Omega."

"Nice," Grayson said as he gave Alex a fist bump.

I knew that a palindrome is a word like "racecar" or a phrase like "Madam, I'm Adam" that's spelled the same backward or forward. But I had never heard of Palindrome Games. It turns out it's a software company that designs word games that can be played on social media.

When we walked into their office, I thought Grayson was going to faint. It was total compu-geek heaven. There were electronic gadgets everywhere and a handful of programmers working on computers with giant monitors. As far as offices go, it was supercasual. One wall was filled with the latest video game consoles, and there was a massive cappuccino maker in the corner that made the room smell like a coffee shop.

One of the workers wore a vintage concert tee, another had on a Yankees jersey, and a couple sported

Hawaiian shirts. All of them looked like they'd been putting the cappuccino maker to good use and had gone at least twenty-four hours without any sleep.

"I'm home," Grayson said as he soaked it all in. "*This* is where I belong."

The man in the Yankees jersey got up and walked over to us. "You must be the game testers," he said, offering his hand. "I'm Adam."

"Just like the palindrome," I answered. "Madam, I'm Adam."

He smiled as he shook my hand. "Just like the palindrome."

After some quick introductions, he led us into an office filled with even more high-tech stuff.

"We're not really game testers," Natalie admitted after he'd shut the door.

"I know that," he answered. "But there's no reason for the guys in the other room to know it. Let's just keep that between us Omegas."

"You were an Omega?" I asked.

"Still am," he corrected me. "Omega today, Omega forever. I graduated from MIST nine years ago and started this company when I was a senior at Stanford."

"Impressive," Grayson said, looking around at it all.

"Not as impressive as you four figuring out the riddle in less than three hours," he said. "This morning I got word from the Prime-O that you might be coming soon. But we thought it would take at least a couple days for you to make it here."

We each stood up a little straighter and tried to hide how pleased we were with ourselves, but I think our big goofy smiles kind of gave us away.

"Are you going to tell us what the Baker's Dozen is?" Natalie asked.

"I'm going to do better than that," he said with a sly smile. "I'm going to show you. But first we need to take care of security and I need to scan your handprints."

He plugged a scanner the size of a textbook into his computer and had each one of us press our right palm against it. Then he used the palm prints to create security access for us.

"Okay," he said once he was done. "Let's check out the attic."

"What's the attic?" asked Natalie.

"The attic is what you're looking for," he said somewhat cryptically.

He led us back into the hallway and onto the elevator. Then he pushed the button marked 20.

"Originally, this building was twenty stories high," he explained. "But a year after it was completed, they mysteriously decided to add an additional floor. Everyone calls it the attic."

The elevator door opened, and we stepped out onto the twentieth floor. The entire floor was a little strange. First of all, the layout of the offices was odd. Adam said this was due to the shape of a building. "Without nice square walls, it's hard to make nice square offices," he said. Even stranger are the windows. They're high on the wall so that their bottoms only reach down to your shoulders. If you want to get a good look outside, you have to stand on your tiptoes.

"Funky, isn't it," he said. "It gets weirder. Because the attic was added later, the main elevators don't go high enough. The only way to get there is by taking a separate elevator that just connects the twentieth and twenty-first floors."

We stepped into the other elevator, and the button panel had a scanner like the one in Adam's office.

"Try it out," he said to me.

I pushed the button for twenty-one, and nothing happened. But when I pressed my palm against the glass, the elevator instantly came to life and started carrying us to the attic.

"Cool," I said.

"Isn't it?" Adam agreed. "Believe it or not, it gets cooler."

When we reached the twenty-first floor, we stepped out into a tiny hallway.

"Welcome to the attic," Adam said. "It's all Omega."

We traded looks.

"Seriously?" I asked.

"Well, on paper, it all belongs to Palindrome Games," he explained. "This is where we keep our computer servers. But they also function as the electronic hub for the Omegas. For example, every message to or from the Prime-O comes through here. And each door requires a palm scan."

He led us through a series of rooms filled with computer servers.

"Because the building's a triangle, the rooms have an unusual alignment," he explained as we went through them. "As a result, there is one room that virtually nobody knows about. It isn't even in the blueprints, and it can't be detected from outside."

We reached a door that had another palm scanner. Instead of an office number on the nameplate there was simply the symbol "Ω"—Omega.

"Your palm prints will open this door for exactly three

hundred and sixty-five days," he said. "Why don't you give it a try?"

We all traded looks, and then Natalie pressed her hand against the glass. A bright green light traced its outline, and moments later, we heard the door unlock. She reached for the knob, but before she opened the door, she paused and took a deep breath.

"You know that feeling you get on Christmas morning, right before you unwrap your first present?" she asked.

"Yeah."

She flashed a smile and said, "This is way better than that."

She opened the door, and I think each one of us was surprised. So far, everything that we'd seen in the attic was high-tech and ultramodern. The endless rows of servers looked like something out of a science-fiction movie. But this room was strictly old-school. There was a manual typewriter sitting on the end of an oak table and four wooden file cabinets next to a rolltop desk. Knickknacks sat on dusty bookshelves next to outdated encyclopedias and travel guides.

"Apparently, the room's not just a secret from other people," Alex said as we began to poke around. "It's also a secret from the twenty-first century."

Grayson took in a deep breath and added, "It even smells old."

Despite this, there was something undeniably appealing about it. I imagine it's the same vibe you'd get in the office of a brilliant but somewhat offbeat college professor.

"Welcome to the Baker's Dozen," Adam said, addressing us. "For the next year, you're responsible for monitoring the Unlucky 13. These cabinets are filled with more than a hundred years of observations and information about the original thirteen zombies. You must determine their current identities, which are ever changing, and keep close track of their actions to see if there are any changes to the structure or balance of power of Dead City."

"We're not the only team, though, right?" Natalie asked. "They said something about two others."

"That's right," Adam said with a nod. "There's a team of past Omegas who are responsible for support. I'm part of that team, and among other things, we make sure that the room is secure."

Grayson tapped a key on the manual typewriter and asked, "Who makes sure that we have modern office equipment?"

Adam laughed. "Yeah, you're just going to have to get used to that. Think of this room like it's a research library.

Nothing can be taken out. If you generate new reports, they are to be typed on the manual typewriter and not on a computer where they could be hacked."

Natalie gave me a sideways look. "What have you gotten us into, Molly?"

"I'm so sorry," I said.

"Don't be," she replied.

"Yeah," added Alex. "This is awesome."

"Agreed," said Grayson.

"You said there was another current team?" I asked Adam.

"Yeah," he said. "But to be honest, they've been a disappointment. This assignment is not easy. They've struggled to identify the Unlucky 13's current identities, and I haven't seen them in months. That's why we needed to add another team."

"So I guess that means it's up to us," Natalie said.

"You guys solved the riddle in three hours," he reminded us. "I think you'll be up to the challenge. I've got to get back to work. Let me know if there's anything you need."

We said our good-byes, and Adam left us in the room to explore.

We started looking into the different file cabinets. Each one of us took a different one and called out whenever we found something that seemed particularly interesting.

Grayson found an envelope that had photos of eight of the thirteen. They were mostly the same pictures I'd found in the *Book of Secrets*, but this was the first time the others had seen them. He spread them out on the table.

"You were right," Natalie said, pointing at one of them. "That is the guy who died on the subway, Jacob Ellis."

The boys looked and nodded their agreement.

"Check it out," exclaimed Alex a few minutes later. "You know how Adam said this floor was mysteriously added one year after the building was completed?"

"Yeah."

"It gets even more mysterious than that."

He carefully laid a piece of yellowed paper on the desk.

"This is on White House stationery," he announced quickly, getting our undivided attention. "It instructs the builder to add one floor to the top of the Flatiron with enhanced security for the sole exclusive use of the United States Secret Service. It's signed by President Theodore Roosevelt."

"That's strange," I said.

"I think if we look around here some more," Natalie said, "we'll find all kinds of strange and unusual things."

"Like this," Grayson said, holding up an aged ledger.

"This has a section for each of the thirteen. And in that section, it lists sightings, locations, known addresses, and so on."

He flipped through the pages, which were filled with handwritten notations and dates going back to the early 1900s.

"Now, look at this section," he said.

He turned it to the final tab. The name on the top of the page was Milton Blackwell. Everything beneath it was blank.

"How are we supposed to find a guy who nobody's seen for over a hundred years?"

8

The Three Wise Men

Blackwells are strong. Blackwells survive. Blackwells are strong. Blackwells survive."

The phrase kept repeating in my brain until it was drowned out by a steady throbbing in my ears that distorted all sound. I could tell someone was talking to me, but I couldn't understand the words. Then, after a few moments, I was able to make out a voice calling my name.

"Milton, can you hear me? Milton, are you alive?"

Time seemed to bend as my mind raced back and tried to piece together what had just happened. In one flash of memory, I could see the fuse burning its way toward the explosives.

In another, I caught a glimpse of the blast in slow motion, a million tiny pieces of rock heading right toward us. That's when I realized that I was still in the subway tunnel. I bolted upright and cried out, "Oh no! What have I done?"

And so it happened that the last words I said while I was alive were also the first ones I said once I became undead. The mind is a funny thing, and in trying to make sense of the incomprehensible, it had replayed the last moments before the explosion, trying to undo my mistake.

"You're alive," said the voice. "Thank goodness you're alive!"

I looked over and realized that the voice belonged to my brother Marek, who had also survived.

Or so I thought. So we all thought.

One by one, as my brothers and cousins regained consciousness, they all arrived at the same conclusion. They had cheated death. Each one was sure that he'd been spared by some miraculous twist of fate. But unlike them, I had done the computations and understood the magnitude of the blast. I was certain that fate alone could not explain it.

"That's impossible," I said as I pulled myself up from the rock and debris. "The explosion was too strong. Every law of science dictates that we should be dead."

Marek laughed. "That's the problem with your books and

equations, brother. You believe them more than you believe your own eyes. Look around. We're all alive. And not only that, but do you see what your explosion did to that black devil?"

I turned toward the rock face and could not believe my eyes. The massive bedrock that we had battled for weeks was gone. The impenetrable wall of Manhattan schist had been reduced to a pile of crushed rubble that sparkled with flecks of orange and green.

A momentary wave of relief washed over me.

"I did it?" I asked in stunned amazement. "My explosives broke through the rock?"

"Yes," he said gleefully. "You brought the devil to his knees!"

I turned to embrace Marek and celebrate, but that's when I noticed that something was wrong. His left arm was bent completely behind his back and twisted in an odd corkscrew. It seemed humanly impossible.

"Your arm," I gasped.

I expected him to scream in agony when he realized what had happened. But he didn't seem pained at all. He just looked at it curiously and simply untwisted his arm and snapped it back into its proper place.

"How did you do that?" I asked.

He thought about it for a perplexed moment and answered, "I have no idea."

The tunnel was dark, but what little light there was reflected in glimmers of orange and green along his cheeks. I saw the same phenomenon on my hands, and when I looked closer, I realized that the light was reflecting off of tiny crystal shards of the schist that had imbedded into my skin.

As the thirteen of us congregated and surveyed one another, we quickly discovered other injuries that defied explanation. The jaw of my brother Elias had detached and dangled from the bottom of his face. Still, he was able to pop it back so that it worked perfectly. Several cousins had fractured bones that had broken through the skin yet somehow caused no pain. And my brother Bartlett was able to walk among us despite the fact that a pickax was buried deep into the middle of his chest. In addition to these injuries, all of us were covered with the glistening shards of rock.

Marek asked me if I knew any scientific explanation for what we were experiencing.

I shook my head and said, "No."

I thought back to when I was a child and had been trampled by the horse. Somehow, Marek had instinctively known what to do that day. So I looked to him again. We all did. He was our leader.

"What should we do?" I asked him. "Where do we go?"

Marek had always trusted family above all else. That's how he selected where to carry me when I was near death as a child, and that's what drove his thinking now. He decided that we would go to our grandfather, Augustus Blackwell.

Before we exited the tunnel, we did our best to mend the most obvious injuries so that we wouldn't attract attention. Then, under cover of night, we traveled to what is now known as Roosevelt Island but which at the time still bore our name.

In 1896, Blackwell's Island was no longer farmland belonging to the family, but our grandfather still owned a large portion of it, and he lived in the same two-story house as his father and grandfather had lived in before him.

That night, of course, we had no idea that our continued survival was directly related to our proximity to Manhattan schist. It was simply our good fortune that Blackwell's Island was formed on the same bedrock. Had our grandfather lived in Brooklyn or Queens, we would have all died the moment we crossed the East River.

As it was, one of us was almost killed anyway.

It was a cold, moonless night, and by the time we reached the house, it was nearly three in the morning. Our grandfather was awakened by the alarming sound of thirteen dazed and confused men walking along the old dirt path in the woods behind his home.

Considering Blackwell's Island was also home to a large prison with frequent escape attempts, it is understandable that he was concerned for his safety. He came out onto his back porch, carrying a lantern and a shotgun. When we emerged from the woods, he was startled by our appearance and aimed the gun at the one leading the way, Marek.

"Grandfather, no!" I shouted out to him. But it was too late. He'd already pulled the trigger, and the bullet ripped right through Marek's chest.

When he raised his lantern and looked closer at our faces, he realized what he'd done and rushed to Marek's aid.

"I didn't know it was you," he wailed as he ran to him.

But a funny thing happened when he got there. Marek didn't need any aid.

"Hello, Grandfather," he said matter-of-factly as a trickle of green slime drained from the fresh hole in his chest. "It seems as though we have a problem."

Grandfather fainted right on the spot. We carried him into the house, and when he regained consciousness, we moved into the dining room, where we had eaten so many Thanksgiving and Christmas dinners. There we tried to explain something that simply defied all explanation. The only thing that made him somewhat open to our wild claims was the fact that Marek had survived the gunshot with no serious injury.

By sunrise, the man we'd called Grandpa Auggie as children had a plan of action. He wanted us to check into the hospital that was right there on the island.

None of us wanted anything to do with that. Known as the Asylum, the hospital had a notorious reputation for mistreating the mentally ill. Just a few years earlier, the horrors of what happened there had been uncovered in an exposé by a journalist named Nellie Bly, who had posed as a patient.

"We are not crazy," Marek said, his voice rising. "These injuries may defy logic, but they are real, not imagined."

Our grandfather assured us that things had changed dramatically and for the better. The Asylum was now a hospital that treated all patients with top doctors. It was also looking to expand and wanted to purchase family land. Grandpa Auggie told us that he could use this as leverage to get us the best treatment and care.

"You are my blood, and I promise I will protect you to the ends of the earth," he said firmly. "This is where I can make sure that you are treated properly."

Reluctantly, we agreed. That morning the thirteen of us arrived at the main entrance to the hospital, a building known as the Octagon.

Initially, we were given first-class treatment, just as our grandfather had promised. Doctors and specialists ran endless series of tests trying to figure out what had caused our condition. They tried to understand why we had no pulse and felt no pain. They tested our suddenly overdeveloped sense of smell.

They were especially fascinated by the fact that each one of us had an identical scar on our right shoulder. It was purplish blue and in the shape of a crescent moon. It was the only injury consistent among each of us.

But the more tests they ran, the more confused they became. Before long, they seemed to view us not as patients to be treated, but as oddities to be feared. By the third day, we were moved into a large basement ward that was little more than a dungeon with solid rock walls.

The walls, however, were made of Manhattan schist, and the longer we were kept there, the stronger we became. My legs, which had been weak ever since my childhood accident, were suddenly powerful and straight. One time, I saw Marek twist the iron frame of a bed like it was nothing.

The continued exposure also magnified our moods. More than ever, Marek was prone to fits of anger and rage. Many of them were directed at me because he saw me as the cause of the accident.

Eventually, the doctors determined that there was no med-

ical explanation for why we were the way we were and therefore no way to treat us. Instead, a secret panel was created to determine what should be done with us. It was a panel of the so-called "three wise men," who represented the most important sectors of city life. It included the mayor, the Catholic archbishop, and the chief of police, a young man named Teddy Roosevelt, who five years later became president of the United States.

Each one of us was questioned individually by the panel. I spoke with them on three separate occasions and developed an instant kinship with Mr. Roosevelt, who shared my love of science.

It soon became evident, however, that even these wise men didn't know what to do with us. We were beyond explanation and as a result were a threat to society. We began to worry that we'd never be allowed to leave the dungeon. Soon, even our own grandfather stopped visiting us. One day, we heard from a nurse that his construction company had just been awarded a large contract with the city. He had traded our well-being for financial gain.

We felt betrayed and abandoned. And Marek . . . well . . . he just felt empowered.

One day, he stood on top of a table in our dungeon and made an announcement.

"It is time for this to end," he proclaimed. "And for that to happen, I must take charge again. Two times, I have let others tell us what to do. The first was with Milton and his explosives. That mistake is what put us in this condition in the first place."

He paused for a moment, and I felt all eyes beating down on me. I did not run away, but I also did not say anything in my defense.

"The next was when I trusted our grandfather to decide our fate. That mistake is how we wound up where we are. I promise you that I will never let anyone else take control of us again. Trust me and follow me and I will get us out of here and onto a new life."

"How?" asked Elias.

Marek flashed a terrifying smile and signaled the others to come closer. I could not tell if I was still part of the group, so I remained where I was.

Then he told them his deadly plan.

Ω 9

Family Time

I love my sister Beth. I really do. My problem is that I just can't stand her. Scientifically speaking, we both have forty-six chromosomes, twenty-three from each parent. But that means there are also twenty-three chromosomes from each parent that we didn't inherit. And while I haven't run our DNA through a gene sequencer or anything, I'm pretty sure Beth and I each took the opposite twenty-three from Mom and Dad. She got all of the cheerleading, popular, "My life is one big teen soap opera" chromosomes, and I took all the, you know, lame ones.

And it's not just that we don't have anything in common. It's that almost every conversation turns into an argument. Anytime one of her possessions is not in the exact location she expects it to be, I get the blame. I mean, just because I borrow her clothes every once in a while doesn't mean I want all of her junk. Still, there she was storming into my room, making an accusation.

"Where's my phone?" she demanded.

At the time, I was trying to figure out why my Internet connection had gone down, so I was too busy to bother turning around. I just kept clicking the reconnect button and answered, "How should I know?"

"Because you took it."

See what I mean? Every time.

"I didn't take your stupid phone," I said, still without giving her the satisfaction of eye contact.

"It was recharging on the counter, and now it's gone," she continued. "If you didn't take it, then what happened to it?"

"I don't know," I replied. "Maybe it got sick of listening to your idiotic conversations and threw itself out the window. Or maybe it died of embarrassment because of that stupid pink case you put on it. But I have no idea where your phone is."

"I'm going to count to ten, and if you don't give it to me, I'm going to I tell Dad."

"All the way up to ten?" I said. "You need help with that math?"

We gave each other dueling stink eyes for a second, and then both of us raced toward the kitchen. In these situations, it's essential for me to reach Dad first, before Beth can start filling his head with misinformation. Unfortunately, she beat me to the door and then butt-blocked me the entire way down the hall. When we got to the kitchen, Dad was getting ready to make dinner.

"Dad," Beth whined. "Molly took my phone and won't tell me where it is."

"Dad," I said at the exact same time. "Beth always accuses me of stuff, and there's never any evidence. It's not fair."

"Time-out," he said, making a *T* with his hands. "Let's settle down. We'll get to the phone and the accusations in a moment . . . but first things first. . . . Is this new apron too frilly? Or am I pulling it off?"

"Dad?!" we both whined in unison.

"Okay, okay, we'll skip my problems and work with yours," he said. "Let me get this straight. Beth, your phone is gone?"

"Yes."

"But if it's gone," he said in his goofy, over-the-top way, "then how will you text anyone?"

Beth completely missed the sarcasm. "That's the problem. I can't."

"O-M-G," he replied.

"Wait a second," she said, finally getting it. "*You* took my phone?"

"Y-E-S."

I folded my arms and gave her my best self-righteous look. "I'll just wait here for my apology."

Instead of an apology, I got attitude. "You know, you'd look more like a victim of unfair accusations if you weren't wearing *my* sweatshirt."

I looked down at what I was wearing and realized I'd been busted. But of course I wasn't going to admit to that. "I thought this was a family sweatshirt," I offered lamely. "For all of us to wear."

"There's no such thing," she said.

Then it occurred to me that if Dad took her phone, then maybe . . .

"Does that mean you have something to do with the Internet being down too?" I asked.

"I don't know," he said. "Would disconnecting the

104

router and hiding it in the same spot where I hid Beth's phone make the Internet go down?"

I sighed. "Yes, it would."

"Then yes, I had something to do with that, too," he answered. "It sounds like I've been pretty busy. But on the plus side, the three of us now have some free time to hang out. You know . . . like a family."

Beth and I both made identical groans. (Okay, so maybe we have a couple of genes in common.)

"Do we have any choice in this?" Beth asked.

"Of course you do," he said. "I'm not some evil dictator. I'll let you decide what we're going to do."

"What are our options?" I asked.

"Well, we can make dinner together, eat dinner together, and talk to one another during the whole time we're making and eating dinner."

"Or?" Beth asked, clearly unimpressed with option one.

"Or," he said, "we can go to your grandmother's house, and I can show you how to massage her calves and pumice the calluses on her feet. Totally your choice."

Beth almost laughed, but she was trying to prove a point, so she wasn't going to give in that easily. "I should call your bluff and pick Grandma," she said.

Now Dad laughed. "If you don't think I'd go through

with it and make you actually chisel those suckers down, well, then you haven't been paying attention for the last seventeen years."

I needed no more convincing than that. "I vote dinner."

"That's my girl," Dad said. "What about you, Beth? Care to make it unanimous?"

"Okay, but I want to go on record as saying that you, in fact, are nowhere near pulling that off," she said, pointing at his apron.

"That's what I thought," he said as he took it off and handed it to her. "I guess that means you'll have to wear it and take the lead."

"Sucker," I said, pointing at her.

"Normally, I don't condone taunting," he said, giving me a high five, "but she did walk right into that."

That night, Beth and I learned how to make crawfish jambalaya with maple butter cornbread. Of course, you don't just learn a recipe with Dad. There's a whole production that goes into it. In fact, there are a few things that are guaranteed to happen anytime you cook with him.

Most important, you're going to end up with an incredible meal. I'm not just saying this because he's my dad. He's an amazing cook. He can take something simple like spaghetti and turn it into the best meal you've ever had. But along the way you're going to have to put up with goofy accents that are directly related to the food. That means while he's making the life-changing spaghetti, he gives you a lot of "Molly, that's-a not-a da way to make-a da meatball."

Finally, no matter what he's making, there will be one point during the meal when he drops the accent, gets serious, and claims that this one particular food provides the key to understanding the universe. He'll literally say, "You see, Molly, a peanut butter sandwich is just like life," or "Girls, if you can figure out what toppings to put on a pizza, you can figure out how to make the world a better place." (For the record, the peanut butter sandwich is like life because sometimes the simplest things provide the most enjoyment, and pizza toppings teach you the value of diversity, bringing out the best in all of us.)

This night was no exception. The jambalaya was incredibly good, and the ridiculous Cajun accent was incredibly bad. (Funny but bad.) And how is jambalaya like life?

"Look at all the ingredients," he said a few bites in. "It has crawfish, sausage, peppers, onions, rice, all with unique tastes. But if you add just a little bit of hot sauce, the taste of all those things changes. It's amazing how just a little bit of something in the right place can change the world around it."

"That's really deep, Dad," Beth mocked. "Color me amazed."

"Yeah," I added. "You just changed my entire outlook on life."

"You tease, but you know I'm right."

Also amazing was the fact that Beth and I had spent more than two hours together without a single disagreement or accusation. It took her a little while to warm up to the whole cooking idea, and it was a struggle for me to chop okra with a cast on my hand, but we laughed a lot, caught up with one another's lives, and had a really nice time.

When we were done, Dad reached into a drawer and pulled out Beth's phone and the router.

"Before I give these back," he said, dangling them in a tempting manner. "There's a new policy in the Bigelow house."

Beth and I both started to moan, but he cut us off.

"Just hear me out," he said. "You're both busy with school and friends, and that's great. And I work crazy hours, and that's not going to change. But in the old days, Mom used to take care of this. She would plan little day trips for us that we all enjoyed."

"Like the zoo," I said.

"Or the time we went to that corn maze," Beth said with a laugh. "And we got lost in the maze."

"And then again on the drive home," added Dad.

"Those trips were great," I said.

"Yes, they were," Dad agreed. "So, like it is with most things regarding your mother, it's going to take all three of us to accomplish what she did by herself."

"What do you mean?" I asked.

"I want us to make time to do one special thing together every week or so," he said. "It doesn't have to be big or long, but it has to be together. And we'll take turns planning them."

I was game, but I wasn't sure Beth would go for it.

"What qualifies as special?" she asked with a slight hint of attitude.

"Anything I do with the two of you is special to me," he answered, totally melting away her resistance.

"Okay," she said as he gave her phone back to her. "It sounds great."

Ω 10

The Whole Enchilada

Sometimes Omega work can be scary, like when you're locked in hand-to-hand combat with a completely unhinged Level 3 zombie who's intent on killing you. And sometimes it can be nerve-racking, like when you're hiding in an abandoned catacomb and holding your breath so that you don't make a noise and get discovered. But what I never would have imagined is that sometimes Omega work can be really . . . boring. I'm talking mind-numbingly, eye-glazingly, fall-asleep-in-the-middle-of-a-sentence boring. But that's exactly what it was the first two weeks we worked on the Baker's Dozen.

Every day after school, we went to the secret room in the attic of the Flatiron Building and—get ready to be totally jealous—we sorted papers. (I know. You wish you were me right now, don't you?)

Natalie is something of an organization freak, so we sorted through more than a hundred years of notes, newspaper clippings, logbook entries, and other really dull things so that we could create a two-page document she named "The Whole Enchilada." Her idea was that since we weren't allowed to take anything out of the room, we needed to cram the most important information into something small enough to memorize.

"You realize you're ruining one of my favorite foods by calling it this," Alex protested one day. "Now, instead of cheesy deliciousness, the word 'enchilada' makes me think of endless paperwork. I hope that makes you happy."

"Yeah," she said, not missing a beat. "It kind of does."

Grayson had a problem with it too. But it had nothing to do with the name and everything to do with the lack of technology. "This floor is filled with state-of-the-art servers. With that much computing power at our fingertips, we could digitize these files and cross-reference them a million different ways. It would be faster and better."

Natalie held firm.

"The instructions were specific," she replied. "Adam told us we could only use the manual typewriter that came with the room. So that's what we're going to do. Besides, there's something to be said for using the processing power in our heads. By going through the information and analyzing it ourselves, we might find something that a computer would miss."

Grayson gasped at the mere suggestion. "I'll just pretend you didn't say that."

Despite these protests, everyone whose arm wasn't in a cast took turns at the typewriter, and "The Whole Enchilada" began to take shape. An entry was typed for each one of the Unlucky 13. The first three were the easiest, because they were the ones we already knew were dead.

1. **Marek Blackwell**: Deceased

   Occupation: Consultant, NYC Sandhogs Local 147

   Aliases: Marek Bedford, Marek Fulton, Marek Linden, Marek Nostrand, Marek Driggs

   Most Recent Home: Lower Manhattan near City Hall

   Role within the 13: Mayor of Dead City

   Last Sighting: Pushed from the top of the George Washington Bridge

2. **Cornelius Blackwell**: Deceased

   Occupation: Laborer

   Aliases: Cornelius Hayes, Cornelius Buchanan, Cornelius Fillmore

   Most Recent Home: Greenwich Village

   Role within the 13: Marek's enforcer

   Last Sighting: Killed by Molly in the St. Andrew's Prep locker room

3. **Jacob Blackwell**: Deceased

   Occupation: Jeweler

   Aliases: Jacob Long, Jacob Staten, Jacob Ellis

   Most Recent Home: Roosevelt Island

   Role within the 13: Unknown

   Last Sighting: Found dead, handcuffed on the R train in Brooklyn

Natalie sat at the typewriter and began the next entry. "Ulysses Blackwell, "she said. "What can you tell me about good old Ulysses?"

"He should be rich," I said, looking at a logbook. "He's always worked with money, either at banks or on Wall Street."

4. Ulysses Blackwell: Deceased

Occupation: Banker/Finance

"Occupation: banker slash finance," Nat said as she typed in the information. "What aliases has he used?"

I had the slips right in front of me. "Ulysses *Hudson* worked as a teller for the First Chemical Bank in the 1940s. Ulysses *Cabot* was a trader on Wall Street in the seventies. And Ulysses *Drake* was president of a small bank near Lincoln Center as recently as 2005."

"Look at that: He went from bank teller to bank president, and it only took him sixty-five years," Grayson said. "I guess if you live forever, you really can get ahead in this world."

Aliases: Ulysses Hudson, Ulysses Cabot,

Ulysses Drake

Next, she turned to Alex. "Where's the last place we know that he lived?"

Alex was sitting cross-legged on the floor, surrounded by stacks of files that looked totally random but somehow made sense to him. He ran his finger along one of the piles and pulled out a sheet of paper like a magician pulling a rabbit out of a hat.

"According to this . . . nowhere," he said as he double-checked the paper. "The Omegas have never been able to confirm a home for him."

Most Recent Home: Unknown

"However, we do have a picture," Grayson said, holding up a photo. "And judging from the really ugly polyester suit he's wearing, I'm guessing that if he is rich, then he's not spending his money on nice clothes."

"What's it say on the back?" Natalie asked.

Grayson turned the photograph over and read the caption. "May 25, 1977, Ulysses Blackwell wearing an ugly suit in Columbus Circle. Okay, I added the part about the suit, but seriously?" He held it up so I could see.

"I'm with you," I said. "I think calling it ugly is being generous."

Natalie went back to the list. "And his role within the 13?"

"Definitely finance," Grayson said. "He's involved with anything concerning money."

115

"And last but not least, where was his most recent sighting?"

"Give me a sec, I have that," I said, going back to my slips of paper. I shuffled through them and found what I was looking for. "According to this observation log in 2005, he was followed from his bank until he disappeared into a crowd in Columbus Circle."

Natalie thought about this for a moment. "Interesting . . . If the picture was taken at Columbus Circle, and the last sighting was at Columbus Circle . . . maybe that's where he lives."

"Maybe," Grayson said. "But there's no way to know that from a picture and a sighting twenty-eight years apart."

"Okay," Natalie answered. "I was just thinking out loud."

"Wait," Alex said as he clapped his hands and let out a woot. "He does live in Columbus Circle."

"Did you unearth another piece of paper in that pile of yours?" asked Nat.

"Nope," he said with a big smile.

"But I thought you said no one's ever been able to confirm an address?" Natalie said.

"*I* just confirmed it."

Grayson and I exchanged confused looks.

"And how did you do that?" I wanted to know.

"His aliases: Hudson, Cabot, Drake," he said. "What do those names have in common? Henry Hudson, John Cabot, and Sir Francis Drake. They're all explorers, just like Columbus. Therefore, Ulysses lives in Columbus Circle."

"That's not confirmation," Grayson said. "It's coincidence."

"No, I think it's a pattern," Alex replied. "What about Jacob Blackwell? Where did he live before he got handcuffed to his seat and died in on the subway?"

"Roosevelt Island," said Natalie.

"And his aliases . . . ?"

"Jacob Long, Jacob Staten, and Jacob Ellis." As she read them off, she made the connection and couldn't help but laugh. "They're all islands! Long Island, Staten Island, Ellis Island, Roosevelt Island."

"Okay," Grayson said, getting into it. "That *is* a pattern."

Natalie thought about it for a moment. "So they're all picking aliases based on where they live?"

"Sounds like it," I said. "What are Cornelius's phony names again?"

"Hayes, Buchanan, Fillmore," she said, looking at the list.

It took only a second for Grayson to solve it. "Presidents. All three were presidents."

"For that matter, all three were bad presidents," Alex joked.

"But Cornelius lived in Greenwich Village," said Natalie, bringing our momentum to a halt. "What do presidents have to do with Greenwich Village?"

We all considered this for a moment.

"Nothing," Grayson said.

"And Marek's names are all streets in Brooklyn," I reminded them. "But since he couldn't leave Manhattan, there's no way he lived in Brooklyn."

We were close. We knew the names followed a pattern. We just weren't quite sure what the pattern meant. We all sat there for a moment trying to figure it out.

"Remind me again: Where did Marek live?" asked Grayson.

"In Lower Manhattan," said Natalie. "Near City Hall."

I laughed.

"What's funny about that?"

"It's ironic that he lived near City Hall," I said, "considering he was called 'The Mayor of Dead City.'"

That's when Natalie made her "eureka" face. "That's it," she said. "That's our mistake."

"What's our mistake?" I asked.

"I wasn't aware that we'd made any mistakes," said Alex.

"We're trying to think of places in New York City," she explained. "But the Unlucky 13 don't live in *New York City*."

"No," I said, getting her point. "They live in *Dead City*."

"That's right," she said. "And in Dead City, you're not looking for landmarks aboveground. You're looking for ones that are underground. You're looking for . . ."

". . . subway stations," Grayson said, finishing her sentence before she could. "Columbus Circle and Roosevelt Island aren't just parts of town; they're also the names of subway stations."

Alex made a noise like a game show buzzer signaling a right answer, and we all crowded around Natalie and looked at the list together.

"Okay, so Jacob lived in Greenwich Village," Alex said. "But there is no subway station named Greenwich Village. The main one there is . . . Washington Square."

"Washington, Hayes, Buchanan, and Fillmore," Natalie said, listing them off. "Presidents all."

Grayson and Alex did a celebratory chest bump.

"And what subway station is at City Hall?" I asked as I started to do a little victory dance of my own.

All four of us answered at the same time, "Brooklyn Bridge."

"So the Brooklyn street names make sense!" I concluded as I spiked an imaginary football.

Suddenly our incredibly dull paperwork didn't seem quite so boring anymore. We kept typing up the Whole Enchilada, and the pattern helped us fill in some blanks. There were still some holes, especially concerning Milton Blackwell, but we now had a much better picture of the Unlucky 13.

Natalie laid the two pages on the table, and we all looked them over. As always, we were trying to find patterns.

"Here's something that doesn't make sense to me," Natalie said. "Why do they live so far apart from each other? You'd think they'd want to be closer so they could help each other out. But they're spread all over Manhattan."

"Maybe we can ask them ourselves," Alex joked. "Now that we've got this part figured out, we get to go out into the field and look for them, right?"

"Yes, Alex," she said. "Now you can stop doing paperwork and go back to doing what you love best . . . hunting zombies."

Alex flashed a huge smile. "It's not so much that I love it. It's just that I'm really good at it."

"Speaking of which," said Grayson, "what's our plan for finding these guys? Are we just going to stand in Columbus Circle and look for a banker in a really ugly suit?"

Now it was my turn to smile. "I think it's time for you guys to meet my friend Liberty."

"You mean the crazy, bald whack job who gives speeches about zombie rights at all the flatline parties?" asked Alex.

"I prefer to call him the 'former Omega who saved my life when I was about to get attacked by a mob and knows more about the Unlucky 13 than any of us,' but yes, I mean him," I said.

"Well, it doesn't matter what you call him," Alex said. "We can't ask him for help. We're only allowed to discuss the Baker's Dozen with people who are part of the project."

"About that," I said as I set a paper down in front of them.

"What's this?" Natalie asked.

"It's the observation log about Ulysses Blackwell going from the bank to Columbus Circle. Look at the signature at the bottom."

She looked at it and smiled. "Liberty Tyree. He was part of the Baker's Dozen."

"Cool," Grayson said.

Alex, however, had a concerned look. "Okay, I get that he saved you, and I believe in the whole 'Omega today, Omega forever' thing," he said. "But I'm just going to say what I think, even if it sounds prejudiced. He's a zombie, and I don't think the undead can be trusted. For all we know, he's a Level 2 and doesn't have a soul or a conscience."

"We can trust him," I said firmly.

Alex went to say something else, but he held his tongue.

"How would we even get in touch with him?" asked Grayson.

"Just like Alex said," I answered. "He gives speeches at every flatline party. All we have to do is crash one of them."

"Didn't Liberty have to save you from an angry mob because your cover was blown at a flatline party?" Alex pointed out. "I don't think it's safe for you to go back down there again."

The thought of them going without me was not good. I didn't want to miss it.

"I didn't have you guys to help me with my makeup," I said defensively. "With your help, I can totally blend in."

Grayson went to say something, but Natalie held up a finger to quiet us.

"Do you all want to hear what I think?" Natalie asked in a way that reminded us that she was in charge.

"Yes," said Grayson.

"Of course," said Alex.

"Liberty might be able to give us some valuable information, so I think talking to him is a good idea," she said. "We should be cautious about it, but it's not like we'll be revealing anything. He already knows Molly's an Omega, and he already knows about the Baker's Dozen."

"What about me and the flatline party?" I asked her.

"I'm with Alex on that one, I don't think you should go," she said, bringing a frown to my face.

"But Liberty doesn't know any of us, so he'll probably only help if you're there," she continued. "We'll just have to make it work."

And there's the smile again.

"We'll do the makeup at my place," she said. "My mom's got a couple of wigs you can try."

I went to protest, but I could tell by her expression that she didn't want to hear it.

"A wig sounds nice," I lied.

"Where did you go down last time?" she asked.

"J. Hood Wright Park," I told her. "Just like we did when we went underground for my final exam."

"You might get recognized if you go to the park again," she offered. "We should probably try a different approach."

"You thinking subway salsa?" Alex asked.

Natalie and Grayson both nodded their agreement.

"Subway salsa?" I asked. "Is it just me or does that sound like the worst Mexican food ever?"

"Come on," Natalie said, ignoring my question. "We better go try on some wigs."

Ω 11

Subway Salsa

Normally, you crash a flatline party by scoping out a group of zombies at a park and then following them into Dead City once they get word of the location. The advantage of this approach is that because the undead are waiting around, they're easier to pick out and follow. But since we were worried I might get recognized at the park, we were piggybacking instead.

"Piggybacking" is when you pick up a group after they're already on the move. To do this, you've got to find an underground location where you can wait around without being noticed but still be in position to move the moment you spot them. That's what brought us to the Times Square subway station.

Not only is it centrally located, but it's also the biggest and busiest station in the entire subway system. That means that no matter where a flatline party is being held, there's a pretty good chance that at least some zombies will have to pass through it on their way. It's also one of the only places in which there are stores actually inside the subway station. This let us stand around without attracting attention. Grayson and Natalie were over at the Smoothie Shack, while Alex and I pretended to browse at a Spanish music shop.

"This place is legendary," Alex said as he flipped through the CDs made by bands I'd never heard of. "It has the best selection of Latin music anywhere."

I looked down and noticed that Alex's feet were moving in perfect rhythm with the music playing throughout the store.

"What's that?" I asked, pointing at his feet.

Judging by his reaction, I think he was unaware that he'd been doing it.

"Salsa dancing," he said sheepishly.

So that's why they call it subway salsa, I thought.

Alex is always full of surprises, but salsa dancing had to rank pretty high on the "I never would have guessed he could do that" list.

"*You* know how to salsa dance?" I asked, still trying to process it.

"It's not too difficult," he said. "You move on the first three beats and pause on the fourth. Like this."

He demonstrated the steps for me, and they seemed as fluid and natural as could be. It was like he was on one of those TV dance shows.

"And you know this . . . how?"

"I have three sisters, and they all take dance," he said. "Who do you think gets to be the partner in all of their living room practice sessions?"

I laughed and realized this was just one item on the endless list of things that made Alex awesome. Of course, I was still going to give him a hard time about it. But before I could do that, Natalie and Grayson appeared at the entrance and signaled us to follow them.

It was piggyback time.

"We've got six on the move," Nat said once we caught up with them. She nodded toward a group about fifteen feet in front of us. We stayed with them but made sure not to get too close or do anything that might attract attention. All of us, that is, except for Grayson, who took a loud slurp from a bright pink smoothie.

We all stopped for a moment and looked at him.

"Seriously?" Alex asked.

"It's Caribbean Delight," answered Grayson with a big smile. "It has coconut, strawberry, and banana. It's delicious."

"It's also distracting," Alex said. "Get rid of it."

"No way," Grayson protested. "Do you know how much this cost?"

"Fine," he replied, "then hurry up and drink it."

"If I hurry," Grayson said. "I'll get brain-freeze."

Before Alex could get too frustrated, Natalie took charge of the situation.

"Let's just focus here," she said. "Grayson, just drink it quietly."

He nodded and took a silent sip as if to demonstrate that he could do just that.

"Perfect," she said.

We followed the group as they moved through the station. It sprawls for blocks in every direction, and they covered a lot of ground before they came to a stop on the southbound platform. There, they blended in with the crowd, and we got in position so that we could board the train a few cars behind them. But when the train pulled up and everyone started to get on, we noticed that they were staying on the platform.

We stopped cold, which of course means we got bumped into a few times, and we fought against the flow of traffic to keep from getting on. There was no way we could have just stood on the platform without attracting their attention, so we tucked in behind a stairwell where they couldn't see us. Luckily, Alex spied a large security mirror set up above the track. Their image was a little distorted by the roundness of the mirror, but we were able to watch them in total silence until . . .

Slurp.

All eyes turned to Grayson again. He swallowed a gulp of smoothie before mouthing the word *sorry*. Alex and Natalie shook their heads and turned their attention back to the mirror.

"Where'd they go?" Alex said. "They're gone!"

I looked up at the mirror, and sure enough, there was no sign of them.

We came out from behind the stairwell and scanned the entire platform. We were all alone.

"How is that even possible?" asked Natalie. "Did they get down onto the track?"

"No way," Alex said. "We would have still been able to see them."

"How do six zombies just disappear?" I asked.

"It was not because of my smoothie," Grayson added defensively.

We walked down to the end of the platform and were surprised to discover a large metal cover in the middle of the concrete floor.

"I don't believe it," Alex said, shaking his head.

"Is that some kind of trapdoor?" I asked.

He nodded. "I think it is."

"If so, we'll have to wait until after the next train to see," Natalie pointed out as another wave of commuters soon filled the platform, making it impossible for us to lift the door without being seen.

I looked across the tracks and noticed something interesting. Normally, the northbound and southbound platforms of a subway are directly across from each other, so there's almost always somebody waiting on one side or the other. But at Times Square, the platforms are staggered a block apart, so when one empties out you get a little privacy before the next crowd comes along.

Sure enough, a few minutes later, everyone but us piled onto the train, and we were all alone for a moment. Alex reached down, flipped up a handle, and pulled.

"It *is* a trapdoor," Grayson said as he peered into the darkness below.

We each entered and went down the small flight of stairs. Alex was the last one through, and he closed the door behind him. We stepped into an abandoned station that was laid out with tracks going east and west instead of north and south like the one above.

"I've never seen this ghost station before," Natalie said as she looked around at our surroundings.

"Me neither," added Grayson. "And I'm kind of wishing I wasn't seeing it now."

The first time I'd crashed a flatline party, it was in an ornate ghost station that had beautiful tile mosaics, brass chandeliers, and stained-glass skylights. This one was not like that at all. It was filled with trash and garbage and had graffiti painted on all the walls and floors. In other words, it was downright scary.

"Hear that?" Alex asked, referring to the thumping beat of house music coming from the darkness. "The party is close by."

Sure enough, we followed the sound and hadn't walked very far before we came across a small crowd of zombies heading for the party. We slipped right in behind them and acted like we belonged. Pretty soon, we were zigzagging through ancient basement hallways until everything slowed down and we realized we were at the end of a line waiting to get in.

"Check it out," Grayson said, pointing to the wall where NEW YORK TIMES was painted on a faded metal sign. "We're still close to Times Square."

I nodded.

"Why is it so backed up?" Alex asked the man standing in front of us.

"Security," he said.

We all exchanged confused looks.

"Security?" I asked.

"You know," the man responded. "They want to make sure no breathers try to get in. There's been a problem with that lately."

Suddenly I felt very nervous.

"Relax," Natalie whispered, sensing my fear. "It's dark, and your wig and makeup both look good. We'll be fine."

This calmed me until we reached the next corner and turned. Ahead of us, we could see the doorway to the party. Two massive Level 3s were standing guard while another two slightly smaller but no less intimidating ones were checking each person's ear before they were allowed to go in.

"Is that what I think it is?" I asked, referring to the small white object each guard was holding.

Alex looked at it for a moment and nodded. "I'm afraid it is."

Relaxing was now out of the question.

The guards were holding ear thermometers like the ones doctors use to check your temperature. But, unlike my pediatrician, they weren't checking to see if anyone had a fever. They were checking to see if anyone had any temperature at all.

The undead have no blood, so they produce no warmth. You'd think the simplest way to tell if someone is living or undead would be to check for body heat. But the problem is that because their sense of touch is so distorted, they can't feel the heat given off by a living person. That's why a zombie can touch you and not know you're still alive. But once those guards put a thermometer into one of our ears, we were bound to be exposed.

My instinct was that we should run. But it was crowded, and there was no way we could without attracting attention. So while I stood there and silently panicked, I gulped. So did Grayson. But his was not so silent.

Slurp.

Natalie snapped her attention toward him, and he cringed.

"Why do you still have that?" Alex asked.

"We got here so quick, I didn't have time to throw it away," he said. "I'll do it now."

He moved to toss his smoothie on the ground with the other trash, but Natalie reached over and stopped him.

"No," she said with a sly smile, reaching for it. "Give it to me instead."

"That's pretty gross," I commented. "You don't know what kind of backwash is in that thing."

"I'm not going to drink it," Natalie said as she looked both ways to make sure no one was looking right at her. "Why don't you guys surround me for a sec?"

We moved in tightly around her to give her as much privacy as we could. Then she put her finger over one end of the straw so that it held some of the smoothie inside as she lifted it out of the cup. Next, she pulled back her hair and put the other end of the straw in her ear. Finally, she released the top of the straw, letting pink goop pour out.

"Okay," I said. "That's even grosser than drinking."

"No, it's not," said Alex. "It's brilliant. You are absolutely brilliant."

Natalie smiled proudly, and I suddenly realized what she was doing. She was lowering the temperature inside her ear. Luckily, it was dark and crowded and we were each able to secretly fill our ears with Caribbean Delight. It felt disgusting and made it hard to hear clearly, but when the

guards put the thermometers in our ears they only measured the ice.

Each one of us was waved in.

"So yay me for buying the smoothie," Grayson said once we'd cleared the entrance and were all trying to clean the gunk out of our ears.

Alex shook his head and laughed. "You got lucky on that one."

The party was being held in a cavernous room the size of a football field. It was filled with the hulking remains of printing presses that stood thirty feet tall and were connected by twisting chutes and conveyors.

"This must have been where they used to print the *New York Times*," Grayson said, marveling at the massive machines.

"Very impressive," Natalie commented. "Now they look kind of like . . ."

"Dinosaurs," I said. "They look like giant metal dinosaurs on display at the Museum of Natural History."

She smiled. "That's exactly right. That's just what they look like."

As we looked for Liberty, we couldn't help but notice that this party had a different vibe than the other ones we'd been to.

"Is it me or does this not seem very party-ish?" asked Grayson.

"It's certainly not you," Natalie said. "The music's dark, the lighting's dark . . . everything is dark."

There was something else very different about this one. Normally, the Level 3s stay off to the side and out of the way, but on this night they were everywhere. Because of the giant printing presses, there was no single main area for the party to take place. Instead, it wrapped in between and around them, making it feel like a maze with Level 3s standing guard at almost every turn.

Despite these differences there were still some things that were just like the other parties. Betty's Beauty Balms were on sale in one corner of the room, and Liberty was giving a speech in another. As usual, most of the people were ignoring him, but (also as usual) he didn't seem to mind. Liberty was determined to get his point across even if he had to do it one zombie at a time.

We waited for the speech to end before we walked up to him.

"Molly?"

"Like my wig?" I joked.

"Not particularly," he said. "What are you doing here? Wasn't last time bad enough?"

"I know," I answered. "But we have to ask you some questions. They're important."

He quickly began to look around. "I can't be seen with you all. Did you notice the security? Things are changing down here. If they think I'm talking to breathers, they'll finish me off."

"See, I told you guys this was a bad idea," Alex said. "Let's get out of here."

Natalie shot him a look and turned to Liberty.

"We need to ask you about the Baker's Dozen," she said.

This caught Liberty off guard, and he wasn't sure what to say. "I . . . I just can't talk about that. . . . Not here."

I followed his gaze and saw that he was looking at a pair of Level 3s who were eyeing us suspiciously.

"Then we'll talk somewhere else," I said. "At the waterfall. Meet us there in an hour."

When he had rescued me at the last flatline party, we'd escaped in the aqueduct, all the way to Morningside Park, where there's a waterfall. He thought it over for a moment before answering.

"Two hours," he said. "I'll get there if I can."

He didn't give us a chance to disagree. He just stormed past us, making a point to push Grayson out of the way as he did.

"Hey," Grayson complained, turning toward him. "What was that for?"

"Them," I whispered as I nodded toward the Level 3s who'd been watching us. They seemed satisfied and finally turned away.

"I don't know about you guys," Natalie said. "But I want to get out of here. Right now."

No one disagreed.

12

A Walk in the Park

T he question came from out of the blue, but it tells you everything you need to know about Alex.

The four of us were standing on the heights that overlook Morningside Park because, despite my many assurances, he still didn't trust Liberty. It was five minutes before we were supposed to meet him, and Alex was still worried. He wanted us high enough to see the entire area around the waterfall so that we could make sure Liberty was alone when he got there.

"I can't stress how dangerous it is for Omegas to arrive anywhere according to a schedule," he reminded me as he scanned the park. "That's especially true at night in an area surrounded by trees. There are so many potential dangers."

I didn't know how Grayson and Natalie felt about it all, but I was frustrated. And to be honest, I was a little offended. We were the ones who had asked Liberty to help us, and yet I felt like we were treating him like the enemy.

"Liberty doesn't have any friends waiting in the bushes to jump us," I said with some attitude. "I don't even think he has any friends. You know, the fact that someone's a zombie doesn't automatically make them evil. The sooner you realize that, the better."

"Hey . . ." Natalie started to protest.

I instantly regretted what I said, and when I saw the hurt look on Alex's face, I wished I could take it all back. This was a sensitive issue for him. Sometimes we kid him about his attitude toward the undead, but I think he worries that we think he's prejudiced.

"I'm sorry," I said, starting to apologize. "I shouldn't have . . ."

He held his hand up to stop me. That's when he asked me the question.

"If we were a rock band," he said, "who would I be?"

I'm sure the bewildered look on my face hinted that I had absolutely no idea what he was talking about. I looked to Natalie and Grayson, and they seemed equally perplexed.

"If the four of us were in a rock band," he said, motioning to us all, "which band member do you think I'd be?"

"I'm sorry," I said, still confused. "I don't understand the question."

"Natalie's the lead singer," he said with a nod toward her. "She's our leader. She's our voice. The other day at the hearing, she spoke for us, and she was brilliant. That's because she's the one who knows the perfect words to express what we're all about."

"Thank you," Natalie said with a pleased smile.

"And me?" I wondered, a bit worried by what he might say.

"That's easy. You're the lead guitar." He answered this as though he had thought through it more than a few times. "You're the musical prodigy who gives us flair and shreds up the stage. You don't even need words to speak. And every now and then, you're the one who gets the huge solo because, quite frankly, we just can't keep up with you."

I smiled and may have even blushed a little.

"Please don't make me the guy who drives the tour bus," Grayson said, perhaps only half joking.

"No, you're the bass player." At this point he pretended

to play a little air guitar, coolly slapping the strings of an imaginary bass. "People who aren't into music don't get how important the bass is, but it's essential. You're under-rated and stand off to the side, but you give us our rhythm. You provide our moral center."

Now Grayson started slapping an imaginary bass too.

"So I'm guessing that makes you the drummer."

"That's right," Alex said proudly. "I'm the drummer. I'm the one who sits in the back and keeps an eye on every-one else. I don't sing. I don't do solos. My job is to make sure you all stay on course. I make sure that you don't get so caught up in the moment that you lose track of the beat. And when some crazed fan tries to mess with one of you, I'm the one who throws the punch that protects you."

"Hey," I said with mock indignation. "I can throw a punch for myself."

"Sure you can," he answered as he tapped my cast. "And you've got the broken bones to prove it."

That made me laugh.

"We're not up here because I don't trust you," he con-tinued. "And we're not up here because I don't trust Liberty. We're up here because I don't trust *anyone*. I can't risk it. You guys make great music, and it's my job to make sure you get to keep playing."

"Well . . . I really am sorry about what I said," I told him.

"Apology accepted."

"You know, the really good drummers get solos too," Natalie pointed out.

He cracked a smile. "Maybe once in a while."

I looked down at the park and saw Liberty walking toward the waterfall. He wore a hoodie and a leather jacket, but even in the darkness, I could tell it was him.

"And just like I promised, he's all alone," I said with an "I'm so proud of myself" smile that lasted the entire ten seconds it took for me to see the four zombies taking their places and hiding in the bushes.

"I don't believe it," I said, turning toward Alex. "You were right."

But just when I expected Alex to say "I told you so," he did something completely unpredictable. He started to run down the stairs toward the zombies. Instinctively, we chased after him.

Worried that he hadn't seen the others and was running into an ambush, my voice rang through the park as I called out, "Stop! It's a trap!"

By this point, Alex was taking two or three steps at a time, and none of us could come close to catching him.

The stairs go on forever, and we were only halfway down by the time he reached the ground level and started sprinting toward the waterfall. That's when I looked up and realized what Alex had already figured out.

The four zombies weren't *with* Liberty. They were there to hurt him. I was now close enough to recognize that two of them were the Level 3s who'd been watching us after his speech. And when I'd called out to Alex, it had spooked them into action. They moved from their hiding places and surrounded Liberty. He had a nervous look as he saw that bad guys blocked every escape route.

Well, almost every one.

Realizing he had no chance in a four-on-one fight, Liberty turned around and dived right into the water. The pond at the bottom of the waterfall is small, but it was still big enough to buy him a little time.

More important, it gave Alex some time too. He kept sprinting at full speed while the zombies tried to figure out what to do with Liberty. Two of them jumped into the water at opposite sides so that they could force him back out while the other two waited for him on the bank.

Unfortunately for them, the zombies on the bank were so focused on Liberty, they didn't see Alex coming until the last second.

Now, before I get to the next part, which I'll warn you gets a little gross, I want to explain a couple things about martial arts that you may not know. First of all, most martial arts, like judo and karate, come from Asia and are primarily used in sporting competitions. They have rules and long traditions of sportsmanship that celebrate elegance and grace.

But Alex was trained in Krav Maga, which is not used in competitions and has absolutely no rules. It's a type of street fighting developed by the Israeli Defense Forces. And, judging by what I saw over the next thirty seconds, it's really effective.

The first zombie turned just in time to throw a punch at Alex, only to have him intercept the fist and snap his wrist with a violent twist. They traded a couple of lightning-quick punches, and out of nowhere, Alex knocked him unconscious with a head butt.

Meanwhile, now that Liberty realized he was going to get some help, he stopped trying to get away from the two zombies that had dived in after him and started fighting one right there in the water.

Natalie, Grayson, and I reached the scene just after Alex had knocked out the first zombie and had been jumped from behind by the second. This is when the "no rules" thing came into play. The whole point of Krav Maga is to end a fight as quickly as possible, even if it means using methods some people might call fighting dirty.

As zombie number two tried to squeeze the life out of him, Alex reached back and jammed his fingers up his nostrils. Then he literally ripped his nose off his face. Next, he spun around inside the bear hug, jammed two fingers into each side of the zombie's mouth, and did a move he calls "the double fishhook." I don't even know what he did next because I had to turn away to keep from throwing up.

By the time the rotted flesh had settled and the water stopped splashing, two zombies were dead, the other two had run off into the darkness, and Natalie was helping Liberty out of the pond.

Liberty looked at me and shook his head, water dripping everywhere.

"The first time we met, I ended up riding in the Old Croton Aqueduct," Liberty said to me. "And this time, I wind up fighting for my life in the Morningside Pond. You're not exactly a good-luck charm."

"Sorry," I said sheepishly.

Next, Liberty walked over to Alex and shook his hand. "You, on the other hand, couldn't have been better luck. I can't thank you enough for saving me."

"It's my pleasure," Alex replied. "Omega today, Omega forever."

"I've never seen someone fight like that before," Liberty said. "What do you call that?"

"I know," Grayson said before Alex could answer.

We all looked to him.

"What?" asked Liberty.

"That's what you call a drum solo."

Ω 13

The Undead Calendar

Rather than hang out at the park, where there might have been some more undead bad guys lurking in the darkness, we decided to head back up the stairs to Morningside Heights. We walked for a few blocks, which gave Liberty a chance to air dry and let Alex change our course enough times to be satisfied that no one was following us.

Finally, we found a pizza place across the street from Columbia University that was jammed with college students. In addition to being loud, it was filled with the mouthwatering aroma of pizza dough baking in the oven.

This last part was important not only because it smelled yummy, but also because it masked Alex's and Liberty's scents, which might have been picked up during the fight by the two zombies who got away.

In short, this was the perfect place for us to hide in plain sight.

We slid into a booth in the back, with Alex, Grayson, and Natalie taking the side against the wall so they could watch both doors for any unwanted visitors. I sat next to Liberty and quickly realized that it was going to take more than air for him to dry off.

"Sorry," he said as he used a wad of napkins to mop up the pond water dripping off his jacket and onto the seat.

"It's all right," I replied as I grabbed a couple napkins myself and helped out.

At first, everything about the conversation was awkward. Here we were, an Omega team, sitting down for some slices with . . . a zombie. Of course, we were all careful not to use the z-word in front of him, but that was kind of the problem. We were so worried we'd say the wrong thing, we barely said anything at all. That is, until I broke the ice in typical Molly fashion by sticking my foot in my mouth.

It happened when I handed Liberty a menu and it

dawned on me that getting pizza might be a big mistake. Undead taste buds are totally different from living ones. I'd learned this the hard way when I'd crashed my first flatline party and tried a dollop of that brown paste they call food. It was disgusting and made me gag. But here we were asking Liberty to eat something that probably tasted just as disgusting to him.

"I'm so sorry," I said as I began to stumble over my words. "I'm sure you don't like . . . I mean, this is not the right kind of . . . or rather, we don't need to . . ."

"Is she always like this?" he asked the others. "Or does she sometimes actually finish her sentences?"

"Sometimes," Alex said, "but even then they don't always make sense."

While the others had a laugh at my expense, I took a moment to compose myself and tried again. "What I meant to say is that I'm sorry we brought you here. It's pretty insensitive . . . considering the type of food you normally eat."

He laughed loud enough that a couple people at other tables turned to look.

"You really are one of a kind, Molly," he said. "You've almost gotten me killed. Twice. But the thing you're worried about is insulting me by bringing me to a pizza joint."

150

Now our whole table laughed out loud, including me.

"Well, when you put it that way," I said with a bashful smile.

"Have no fear," he continued. "The pleasures of greasy pizza extend across all taste buds, even those in . . ."—he looked around to make sure no one was listening before he whispered—"my condition."

We placed our orders, and I handled the official introductions. Despite their concerns about him, Liberty quickly won them over with his sense of humor, and the conversation flowed easily once he started talking about his time at MIST. It turns out we had some of the same teachers and many of the same opinions of them.

"What about the principal, Dr. Gootman?" he asked, smiling. "Does he still give the yeast talk on the first day of school?"

"Every year," Natalie said.

"We will eat bread made from this yeast," Alex said, doing his best Dr. Gootman impression. "And in doing so we will continue a meal . . ."

". . . that has included every student and teacher in this school's history," the rest of us said in unison, laughing.

Liberty closed his eyes for a moment and smiled, maybe replaying the memory in his head. When he opened them he pulled a garlic knot from the basket in the middle of the table and held it up with two fingers.

"To Dr. Gootman, to MIST, and to bread," he said.

We each grabbed a knot and joined him in the toast.

"Dr. Gootman, MIST, and bread!" we said as we "clinked" the knots with one another and popped them into our mouths.

"I want to ask you something," Grayson said, "but I'm worried it's rude."

Considering Grayson's total lack of social skills, we were now all worried about his question.

"Okay," Liberty said. "Give it a shot."

"How . . . did you . . . ?"

"Get this big old scar?" Liberty said, tracing his finger along the scar that ran across his bald scalp.

Grayson nodded.

"It was when I undied, as I like to call it."

I would never have asked the question, but I was so glad Grayson had because I desperately wanted to know the answer.

"I was a student right across the street from here," he said, pointing out the window toward the Columbia campus. "And one Friday night I was bored. I didn't feel like doing homework and couldn't find any friends to hang out with. Remembering my days at MIST and the thrill of being an Omega, I thought it might be fun to go to a flatline party. So, like an idiot, I went there alone. I mean, who does that? Right?"

All eyes looked my way.

"What are you looking at me for?" I asked sheepishly, even though I knew the answer. "Go ahead, Liberty, you were saying . . ."

"I was recognized at the party, and someone jumped me from behind and knocked me unconscious," he continued. "The next thing I remember, I was waking up in an abandoned tunnel surrounded by Manhattan schist. I had a big cut across my head, and Marek Blackwell was standing there looking down at me. He said that he was the mayor of Dead City and informed me that I was its newest citizen. He also told me that he wanted to be the one looking at my face when I realized what I had become. When I realized that I would spend the rest of time running from Omegas, just like the undead had run from me when I was one."

The story was chilling.

"That's why you helped me at the flatline party," I said. "You realized the same thing could happen to me."

Liberty smiled and nodded. "I may have seen some of

my stupid self in you that night. Luckily, we got away."

"What did you do next?" Grayson asked, mesmerized by the story. "Did you move underground? Is that what happens? Did you find an abandoned tunnel to live in?"

Liberty laughed. "No, that's not how it works at all. Most undead try to keep the life they were already living. I didn't change much. I tried to act like it never happened."

"You stayed in school?" asked Natalie.

"I was lucky because my dorm room was on the second floor. The undead are usually fine on the bottom three floors as long as we go underground for an hour or so every day to recharge."

"And no one at the college ever suspected anything?" I asked.

"How could they suspect something that they didn't know was possible?"

"What about your parents?" Grayson wondered.

"That's a different story," he said. "I tried to keep it from them, but they seemed to sense that something was wrong. That Thanksgiving we were supposed to visit my grandmother in New Jersey. I kept trying to come up with excuses to miss it, but they said it was a family obligation and that I needed to go. Finally, I had to tell them that I wouldn't survive past the Lincoln Tunnel. It was all very dramatic."

"How did they take it?" Alex asked.

"Not well." He paused for a moment. "It took a while, but my mom eventually came around. Now we spend Saturday mornings together at the farmer's market in Union Square."

"And your dad?" I asked.

Liberty shook his head. "He still won't have anything to do with me."

The look on his face was heartbreaking. We were all quiet for a moment because no one knew what to say.

"But I'm guessing you didn't crash a flatline party just so that you could find out about my family problems," he said, changing the subject. "I believe someone mentioned something about the Baker's Dozen."

Natalie nodded. "Have you ever been to the attic of the Flatiron Building?"

Liberty flashed a big smile. "That would be the attic with the manual typewriter?"

"Yes," she said. "That's the one."

"Yes, I have been there," he said. "Many times."

He sat up a little straighter and looked at each one of us. Then he leaned forward like he was sharing some sort of secret. "I'm guessing you guys have some questions about the Unlucky 13."

155

Over the next forty-five minutes, we ate pizza (which, by the way, was totally delish), and we got an understanding of Dead City that was more detailed than we had ever known.

"First of all," he said, "you've got to realize that most undead don't live underground. The Level 3s do, but the ones and twos usually find a low-lying place on the surface. And most live pretty regular lives. They try to keep their undeadness to themselves."

"If they don't live there," Alex said, "then why does Dead City even matter?"

"The Manhattan schist, for one thing. You've got to go under every day for at least an hour," he said. "But more than that, Dead City is like Chinatown or Little Italy."

We all exchanged completely confused looks.

"How?" I asked.

"In the old days, when the Italians immigrated to New York, their first stop after Ellis Island was Little Italy. That way, they were around people who understood what they were going through and spoke the same language. And even though most of them settled someplace like Brooklyn or the Bronx, they'd still come back to get that really great Italian food or see old friends. And they'd come back to help new arrivals make the adjustment from the Old Country."

"And that's what happens in Dead City?" asked Alex.

"Yeah," Liberty said. "When you're first undead, you go there just to figure things out and find others who can help you. Eventually, you try to create a normal life aboveground. But you still come back to recharge your energy and keep in touch."

"How do the Unlucky 13 fit in?" I asked.

"Well, you've got to go down somewhere, and every bit of underground is controlled by one of them. They split up the island by subway stations, and whichever one of the Unlucky 13 controls the area around a particular station is called the *stationmaster*."

"And they do this for money?" I asked, trying to make sense of it all.

"That's part of it," he said. "You know that stuff they sell at flatline parties, like Betty's Beauty Balms? Well, for every jar of makeup that Betty sells, a little bit of that money goes to the stationmaster. But mostly, it's about trading something you have that they want. For instance, I studied computers at Columbia. So sometimes I get called to help set up new computer systems. And in exchange . . ."

". . . you get to give your speeches about undead rights."

"That's right," he said, nodding. "I get to give my speeches. And when I go underground to recharge, I don't have to crawl around in some dirty old sewer. There's a place I go to that's nice and has good people there."

"Do the 13 all get along?"

"That's hard to say. Just because they're related doesn't mean they're one big happy family," he continued. "Some get along, and some don't. Some work together, and some like to be left on their own. But there is one thing they all have in common."

"What's that?"

"They're all terrified of Marek," he said. "And that's what keeps them from actually fighting station against station. Marek, as bad as he is, keeps the peace."

The four of us shared confused looks.

"So what's going to happen now that he's dead?" Natalie asked.

Suddenly, Liberty turned very serious. "Marek's dead?" he asked, surprised at the news.

"Hadn't you heard?" I asked, assuming news like that would have spread quickly through Dead City.

"Yeah," Alex said. "Molly killed him."

Liberty turned to me. "You saw his body?"

"I saw him fall off the top of the George Washington Bridge."

Liberty thought about this for a moment and shook his

head. "That may explain why things have been changing."

"What do you mean?" asked Alex.

"Dead City's been getting a little rougher around the edges lately," he said. "Like the party tonight, there were way too many Level 3s taking charge for my taste."

"And why would Marek's death cause that?" I asked.

"If he's not there to keep order, some of the others might be flexing their muscle."

"But you said word hadn't gotten around about that," mentioned Alex.

"Just because it hasn't reached me doesn't mean the Unlucky 13 don't know," he explained. "Besides, it won't become official until he fails to show up for Verify."

"What's Verify?" asked Natalie.

Liberty explained that Dead City follows what's known as the Undead Calendar. Even though the Unlucky 13 control the underground, they rarely come out in public. They let others do all their dirty work for them. But once a year, each one of them has to come out for something called Verify.

"They make an appearance at a large public event so that the general undead population can verify that they're still around and still in charge," he said. "They split up the calendar among them. Twelve months, twelve of them, it works out perfectly."

"But aren't there thirteen of them?" I asked.

"There were thirteen in the explosion," he said, "but only twelve who set up Dead City. Even in the world of the undead, Milton's a total ghost. No one knows what happened to him."

I wondered if we would ever be able to find Milton.

"So what will happen when Marek misses his Verify?" asked Natalie.

"That's a good question," Liberty answered. "My guess is that some of the others already know he's gone and have been trying to get things lined up so that they're in position to take charge."

"How?"

"When it's time for Marek to appear, whoever stands up in his place will be the new mayor of Dead City."

"When's his Verify?" Alex asked.

"New Year's Eve," he said. "In Times Square."

The Night of the Three Screams

There were three screams that night. And even though more than a hundred years have passed, I sometimes still hear them in my sleep. Despite this, my most chilling memory of those events is not a scream but a whisper.

"Milton, can you hear me?"

My cousin Jacob was lying on the floor no more than eight inches from me, but his voice was so faint I could barely make out the words. We were under strict orders not to move or speak, so I knew he was taking a risk simply by communicating with me at all. I nodded ever so slightly.

"No matter what happens, you stay with me," he continued.

"And if I tell you to run, do not look back. Do you understand?"

I nodded again, and no doubt the fear in my eyes confirmed that I understood him perfectly. Jacob was warning me about Marek. The same brother who once saved my life was now looking to end it. Tonight was the night he had picked for our escape. It was the night Marek planned to settle all unfinished business.

In the weeks after the explosion, I'd noticed that the thirteen of us started to form two separate groups with distinct personality traits. Today, the undead refer to these as Level 1 and Level 2, with the primary difference being that Level 1s maintain their souls and their consciences while Level 2s do not. In this way, Level 1s act more like the living while Level 2s are more prone to extreme mood swings and unpredictable behavior.

I have come to believe that the deciding factor as to which level someone becomes is directly related to their emotional state at the moment of death. In the seconds before our accident, I realized the explosion was imminent. My final breathing emotions were guilt and responsibility. Marek, however, was standing next to me and saw my reaction. He also knew the explosion was coming, and as a result, he died angry and filled with hate.

Confined to our so-called ward in the dungeon of the hospital, we were surrounded by walls of Manhattan schist, which only magnified these differences. Marek's anger and hate grew. It was directed at the grandfather who had betrayed us, at the three wise men who had condemned us, but most of all at me.

"You put us here," he sneered at me one day. "But of course I am the one who will have to get us out."

His escape plan was inspired by an unlikely source. Since actual doctors rarely ventured down to see us, we were primarily under the watchful eye of an evil man named Big Bill Turner.

Big Bill had no medical education. In fact, he had no real education at all. His training had come from his days as a street fighter with the Swamp Angels, a notorious gang that terrorized the East River dockyards for decades. His role at the Asylum was not much different, only now he kept order by terrorizing patients with brute force and intimidation.

He loved to brag about his criminal past with the Swamp Angels and one day told us the secret of their success. "We used the sewers," he said with a toothless cackle. "It was genius. We'd rob the ships at night and sneak everything we stole through the sewers so the police couldn't find us."

It was this detail that caught Marek's attention. He wondered if the same sewers that protected the Swamp Angels might also be able to protect us. Over the next few days, he took advantage of Big Bill's ego and got him to talk more about his "genius."

With his experience digging tunnels and Big Bill's knowledge of the layout of the New York sewer system, Marek began to envision a life for us beneath Manhattan. One night he laid out his plan for what today is known as Dead City.

"We will make a home out of the underground," he said as he ran his hand along the craggy wall of schist behind him. "The black devil we once feared will now give us power and protection."

"But we're locked in this hospital," Cornelius reminded him. "How will we even make it to the underground?"

"The same way everyone does eventually," Marek said with a laugh. "We'll die."

Two nights later, the nurse brought us our dinner. She was the only person at the hospital who ever treated us with any kindness or compassion. I especially liked that when she brought us our meals, she'd say, "Good evening, gentlemen. It's time to eat." It was the closest anyone came to treating us like we were human.

That night, however, there was no greeting—just the first scream, a horrified shriek followed by the sound of a dinner tray clattering to the floor. Rather than patients, she saw thirteen lifeless bodies strewn across the room. It appeared as if we'd finally succumbed to our mysterious unknown disease.

"Mr. Turner! Mr. Turner! Come quick!"

In keeping with Marek's plan, my eyes remained tightly shut, but I still had a vivid picture in my mind of what it looked like when Big Bill's massive frame filled the doorway and he looked out at the scene that had traumatized the nurse.

"They finally died," he said, no doubt with a smile on his face. "Well, it saves me the trouble of having to kill them."

He walked over and poked at a couple of us with the tip of his muddy boot. Satisfied that we were, in fact, dead, he turned to the nurse and said, "Best go get the doctors."

The brilliance of Marek's plan was that it took advantage of people's prejudices. The doctors were so relieved that we were dead and no longer their problem that it never occurred to them that we could be faking. We had no pulse. We were not breathing. We were dead. They were so happy to be rid of us, they sent us out for burial that night. Our bodies were loaded onto the backs of two horse-drawn wagons, and we slowly pulled away from the hospital.

It was a still night, and for a while the only noises I heard were the sounds of the horses' hooves clopping against the brick road, the creaking of the wooden wagon wheels, and the very unmusical serenades of Big Bill Turner singing Irish drinking songs as he drove one of the wagons. Soon, however, these were drowned out by the evening's second scream.

It was Big Bill.

Marek and Cornelius had risen from the back of the wagon and attacked him. Unlike the other driver who ran away, Big Bill relished the opportunity for a fight.

That was his mistake.

By the time I was out of my wagon, he already lay motionless on the ground. I couldn't tell if he was dead or unconscious, but he was certainly no threat to us.

We knew it would not be long until the other driver made it back to the hospital and raised the alarm about our escape. Search gangs would soon follow. But we had a tremendous advantage. We were Blackwells, and this was Blackwell's Island. We had spent our childhoods visiting our grandfather and playing in the woods around his home. We knew every path and trail by heart.

Even on this moonless night, we could travel at full speed.

"We scatter here and meet up at the dock," Marek said. "If you're late, you'll be left behind on this godforsaken island."

Everyone began to scatter, and I moved to join Jacob, but Marek took me by the shoulder.

"Milton, you come with me," he said.

I tried to hide my fear. "I-I thought the plan was for me to go with Jacob," I stammered.

"The plan has changed," Marek said ominously.

"Then I'll come with you both," Jacob said, coming to my rescue.

Marek glared at him. "He does not need a cousin to protect him when he has a brother."

It was dark, and all I could see of Jacob were the whites of his worried eyes. I knew he wanted to help, but there was nothing left for him to do.

"I'll see you at the dock," I said to him, hoping that it would be true.

"See you there, cousin," he replied as he turned and disappeared into the woods.

Soon, everyone was gone but Marek and me. He was lingering, and I wasn't sure why. I decided to try to win him over with some flattery.

"Your plan worked perfectly," I said. "You are so very smart."

When he laughed, I could see the flash of his white teeth cut through the darkness. "Smart enough to know what you're thinking."

He was standing next to the horse that pulled one of the wagons and ran his palm across his mane. "I remember another horse and wagon," he said.

I nodded. "So do I."

"And do you remember who saved you that day. It wasn't your cousin Jacob."

"No, Marek, it was you."

"Yet you think I would hurt you now," he said, shaking his head.

I couldn't bring myself to say it out loud. Instead, I just nodded.

"Have no fear, Milton. You are still my brother. I am not going to kill you."

I breathed a sigh of relief, although I wasn't completely certain I could believe him.

"But we have work to do, so follow me."

He started walking down one of the paths, but it led in the wrong direction.

"The dock is this way," I said, pointing behind us. "Aren't we going there to meet the others?"

"Eventually," he replied. "But like I said, the plan has changed."

We walked in silence until I heard the alarm sound from the prison.

"Do you think there's a prison escape on the same night?" I asked, amazed at the coincidence.

"No," Marek said. "I'm sure that's for us. The other driver must have alerted them. Now the guards will be searching for us. We must hurry."

We picked up the pace, and I soon realized where we were headed.

"No, Marek," I gasped. "He's our grandfather."

Marek stopped for a moment and turned to me. The hatred in his voice was unmistakable. "He stopped being our grandfather the moment he abandoned us. And tonight he stops being anything to anybody."

"Why bring me along?" I asked. "You know how much I love him. Yet you want me to be part of this?"

"You're not part of this. You are all of this. This is your fault. The reason I am not going to kill you is because I want you to suffer like the rest of us. Your punishment is that you have to live with the guilt of knowing that all of this is your fault. And you'll have to live with the blood of your beloved grandpa Auggie on your hands."

I shook with emotion, and in the distance we heard the bloodhounds of the guards. I didn't know what to do. But I was not going to back down.

"I won't let you hurt him," I said.

He laughed. "In what world do you think you can stop me?"

"In this one," I said.

He looked at me menacingly for a moment and said, "Maybe I spoke too soon about not killing you."

I had no intention of fighting Marek. But I did have a plan. One side effect of our undead state was that I no longer felt the pain of my childhood injuries. My legs had grown stronger, and it turned out that I was fast. So instead of fighting, I began to run.

I bolted toward my grandfather's house as quickly as I could. Marek chased after me, but he could not catch up.

The third scream that night was mine.

"Grandfather! Grandfather!" I screamed as I approached the house and awakened him. "You're in danger!"

Like he did on the day we first arrived, Grandpa Auggie came out on his porch with a gun. This time he fired a couple of shots into the air that attracted the attention of the *bloodhounds. They began to howl and move toward us.*

I looked back at Marek, about twenty yards behind me. He was angrier than I had ever seen him. But he knew that he would not get his revenge that night.

Just before he disappeared like a ghost into the darkness he yelled to me.

"Don't ever let me see you again!"

I haven't.

Ω 15

I Love a Parade…
I Just Don't Like Watching
from the Twelfth Floor

At the risk of sounding like a really bad word problem, I'm going to give you some impressive numbers. This year, more than ten thousand people marched in the Macy's Thanksgiving Day Parade. They sang, danced, and clowned as they waved from twenty-five different floats, performed in twelve different marching bands, and held ropes that kept fifteen giant balloons from floating away. Literally, millions of people stood in forty-five-degree weather to watch it in person. And while most of the people were bundled up and jammed together along the sidewalk, four watched from the comfort of the balcony in Natalie's apartment.

Okay, technically only three watched it from the balcony and one watched on the TV in Natalie's living room, but I could see some of the balloons as they floated by her window, so that should count for something.

"You're missing all the best stuff," Alex said, oohing and ahhing in a lame attempt to lure me out.

"I'm not missing anything," I replied, pointing at the TV. "When you watch in HD, it's like you're really there."

Grayson gave me a look. "But we *are* really there."

I ignored him.

"I thought you were over your whole fear-of-heights thing," Natalie said.

"I'm up here on the twelfth floor, aren't I?" I pointed out. "I don't see any reason to push my luck and dangle from the ledge of the building."

"It's a balcony, not a ledge," Grayson said. "There's kind of a huge difference."

"Just keep looking for Ulysses, okay?" I said.

Ulysses Blackwell was the reason we had gotten up early, fought our way through the crowds on the subway, and met up at Natalie's on a day we should have slept in. According to Liberty, the parade was scheduled to be his Verify. That meant Ulysses was one of the ten thousand participants. So, while the millions of other spectators kept a lookout for their favorite inflatable cartoon characters, we were trying to get a glimpse of an undead banker last photographed wearing an ugly polyester suit in the 1970s.

It was all the more important because Liberty thought there was a good chance that Ulysses might become the next mayor of Dead City. He had a lot of money and power, and that made him a logical choice to replace Marek.

"Would you guys mind sliding that door shut?" I asked as I wrapped a blanket around my shoulders. "It's getting kind of chilly in here."

Their only response was to open it even more.

"Thanks a lot," I said sarcastically.

With its location overlooking Central Park West, Natalie's apartment was in the perfect spot to see the start of the parade. And while the twelfth floor is a little high to see faces clearly, the balcony let us set up a whole viewing station with a telescope, two pairs of binoculars, and a fancy camera on a tripod with a telephoto lens. (And by *us*, of course, I mean the three of them while I offered encouragement from inside.) It looked like the stakeouts you see in detective shows or spy movies. My job was to keep track of the television broadcast and follow parade information that was streaming online.

Plus, I was in charge of making the hot chocolate, so I was contributing.

"There's got to be an easier way to find him," Natalie said, frustrated, as she scanned faces with a pair of binoculars. "The whole point of Verify is to be seen. So the undead must have a way to identify him in the crowd."

"Yeah," Alex said in my direction. "You'd think your buddy Liberty could have helped us out on that."

"He said he didn't know because Ulysses isn't his stationmaster," I reminded him. "Besides, I thought Liberty was your friend now too."

"I like him, but *friend*?" Alex said, half joking, half serious. "It's going to take a little more."

"Let's go over his aliases again," said Grayson, who was working the telescope. "We know he always uses the names of explorers. In the past, he's been Ulysses Hudson, Cabot, and Drake. What other famous explorers are there?"

"It doesn't matter if there's a Ulysses da Gama, a Ulysses de Leon, or even a Ulysses Magellan marching in the parade," Alex said. "The name doesn't help us because there's no list of participants to search through. The only names that are made public are for the different entries, like the floats, marching bands, and balloons."

"Now, if there was a giant Ulysses Magellan balloon,

that would be a pretty big clue," Natalie joked. "There isn't one, is there, Molls?"

I played along and scanned the roster on the computer. "Let's see, we've got Superman and Mickey Mouse, but no Ulysses Magellan."

Then something on the list caught my eye.

"But how about this?" I said, suddenly getting excited. "There is a marching band from Christopher Columbus High School."

They considered this for a moment and nodded.

"That has potential," Alex said. "How soon until they come by?"

"They're the next marching band," I told them as I checked the lineup. "First there's a Mount Rushmore float, then the cast of a Broadway show, and the band is right after that."

Grayson looked down the street to check how close they were. "That should give us about five minutes," he said with a sly smile. "Or, put another way, that should give us plenty of time for One Foot Trivia."

And so began another round of One Foot Trivia, a game invented by, and to date only ever played by, Grayson and Alex, in which they quiz each other while balancing on one foot. According to the rules, the first one to miss a question or lose his balance is declared the loser.

In their boy world, there was no greater challenge. And as pathetic as it is that they get so competitive about trivia, they make it even worse with their nonstop trash-talking.

"You're not worried that the television cameras might catch you losing and broadcast the shame of your defeat across the globe?" Alex taunted.

"No," answered Grayson. "But I am worried they'll get a picture of you crying like a baby."

"Seriously, guys?" I said.

"Name your category," said Alex.

"What else?" Grayson answered. "Macy's Thanksgiving Parade trivia."

Alex flashed his most intimidating look and said, "Gobble, gobble."

They both lifted one foot into the air.

"Let's start at the beginning," said Grayson. "When was the first parade?"

"Too easy, 1924," answered Alex. "Who was the first balloon character?"

"That's what you're going to ask me?" Grayson said as though he were deeply offended. "You think I don't know Felix the Cat?"

"Do you two have to play that on the balcony?" I asked

while trying to mask my nerves. "We're twelve stories high."

They completely ignored me, and Grayson had a little wobble as he asked, "Which character has appeared in the parade the most times?"

"Snoopy," Alex answered, doing some odd sort of flamingo thing with his legs. "By the way, I read that same article you did. I am so in your head. I know your questions before you even ask them."

"I mean it, guys," I said. "Why don't you play Two Foot Trivia instead? It's just as fun and much safer."

"First of all, this is completely safe," Grayson replied. "Second, if we had both feet down, we'd just be asking each other trivia questions."

"Which would be lame," added Alex.

"But isn't that what you're doing now?" I asked.

"No," Grayson said defensively. "Balancing on one foot makes it a sport."

I turned to Natalie. "Can you make them stop?"

"You know my rule about One Foot Trivia," she said as she sipped some hot chocolate and continued to ignore them by looking down at the parade. "I don't get involved in anything that's stupid."

"How many people watch the parade?" Alex asked, resuming the game.

Grayson looked unsure of the answer and took a huge wobble, which I swear was just to get at me. "In person or on TV?"

"In person," Alex said. "Stop stalling."

Grayson thought about it for a moment and answered, "Three and a half million."

"Actually, it's only 3,499,999," Alex said as he pointed toward me. "You know, because Molly's hiding in the living room and doesn't count."

Grayson tried not to laugh, but when he did, he lost his balance and his second foot came down. Alex raised his hands in triumph and started singing some sort of victory song.

"By the way," I protested, "I'm not hiding."

"If you *athletes* aren't too exhausted by your big game, you might want to check out the marching band," Natalie said. "Here they come."

Alex grabbed a pair of binoculars and Grayson used the telescope while Natalie started taking pictures.

"I see band members in furry hats and flag girls," Grayson said, narrating.

"I don't think he's one of the flag girls," Alex said with a laugh.

"Check along the side and in the back for any adults,"

Natalie said. "He might have slipped in with the chaper-ones."

They scanned all the faces of the people with the band and came up empty.

"What do you see on TV?" asked Grayson.

"Commercials," I said weakly.

He looked over his shoulder at me for a moment. "Just like being there in person. Thanks for all your help."

We completely struck out with the marching band, and after that, we also came up empty with a float called "Age of Discovery," which sounded promising as a name but turned out to be about computers, and a group of Shriners riding in antique cars, including a DeSoto, which is a car named after the first European to explore the Mississippi River but was driven by someone who was most definitely not Ulysses Blackwell.

With just a few more floats to go, we were discouraged.

Grayson came back inside to get another cup of hot chocolate. "Maybe we missed him," he said.

"Or maybe this isn't his Verify," added Alex.

I gave him a look. "If Liberty said it's his Verify, then it is. There are still a couple more entries."

"I only see two," Alex said. "The New York Police Department and Santa Claus."

"Are the police marching or on a float?" I asked.

"Both," he said. "Want to take a look?"

The broadcast was showing another commercial, and despite my fears, I felt like I was in the position of defending Liberty. I took a deep breath and stepped onto the balcony.

"Can I have those binoculars, please?" I asked Alex.

"Get back inside," he said. "You don't have to prove anything. I was just playing with you."

"I'm fine," I lied.

"You're shaking."

"That's because it's cold. Can I have them, please?"

The float was designed to be like the Statue of Liberty's torch, with people standing around the flame and waving to the crowd. I used the binoculars to get a close look at their faces.

"Well, I recognize the chief of police," I said, "but I can't tell with the other people. Most of them are looking the other way."

"What about the marchers?" Natalie called out as she took my spot on the couch. "Anything interesting?"

"No," I said. "They're just high school kids."

Grayson put his hot chocolate down on the counter and rushed back out onto the balcony.

"That's it," he said.

Alex and I traded confused looks.

"*What's* it?"

"The kids in high school who volunteer with the police," he said. "They're called *Explorers*."

Suddenly, Natalie was back on her feet, and all four of us were on the balcony.

"Police Department City of New York," Alex said, reading the name from the banner two of the teens were holding. "Law Enforcement Explorer Program."

We all searched the group, looking for Ulysses. Natalie used her telephoto lens to take photos of everyone so we could check them out later. Grayson went back inside to look at the computer and found something online.

"Listen to this," he said, reading an article. "Last month, a donation from a generous benefactor paved the way to break ground on a new learning center for the NYPD's Explorer program. The donor's name is Ulysses Clark."

"Lewis and Clark," said Natalie, identifying the explorer connection.

"Is there a picture with the article?" I asked.

"Yes," said Grayson. "It's small, and he's surrounded by the Explorers, but you can get a good look at him."

Natalie popped back inside for a second and looked at

the picture. "He's definitely one of the guys on the torch."

She went back on the balcony and started snapping pictures of him.

"At least he's dressing better," Alex said, peering through binoculars. "I wonder if he's cleaning up his act so he can become the new mayor of Dead City."

"Yeah," said Grayson. "And it certainly shows off his influence and power that he's hanging out with the chief of police."

Once the float had passed by, we went back into the warmth of the apartment and relaxed. I was sipping some hot chocolate when it occurred to me that Natalie had disappeared into her room for a few minutes. When she came back out, she had changed clothes and was now wearing a dark blue winter coat, a scarf, and a beret.

"Are we going somewhere?" Grayson asked.

"Well, in about an hour, that float is going to reach the end of the parade at Herald Square," she said. "I don't know about you guys, but if there's a chance that he's going to take charge of Dead City, I want more than a picture. I want to follow him and see where he goes from there."

The Mysterious M42
and Track 61

The Thanksgiving parade officially travels for two and a half miles before ending in Herald Square, right in front of Macy's department store. But once the performers reach the finish line, they still have to turn onto Thirty-Fourth Street and continue for a few more blocks before they can park the floats and tie down the balloons. Our plan was to be there when Ulysses Blackwell climbed down from the Statue of Liberty float so that we could follow him and see where he went. The problem was that this area was closed to the public. The only way you could get in was if you were wearing a special admission pin that was given to all the parade participants.

"We're going in there," Natalie informed us as she stood on her tiptoes to get a good look at it all. She said it in that superfocused way she gets when she won't take no for an answer. But, considering none of us had a pin, I didn't see how we could say yes. Talking your way past a guard at the Flatiron Building was one thing, but this place was swarming with security and police.

"You know, I'm really looking forward to Thanksgiving dinner," Alex said, "and I don't want to miss it because I'm locked up in parade jail."

Natalie gave him the death stare. "You don't think we should try to get in there?" she asked in disbelief.

"No," he replied, holding his ground. "I don't."

She considered this for a moment before curtly answering, "Fine. I'll just go by myself."

See what I mean? When she gets this way, there's nothing you can say or do to stop her. She disappeared for a while, and we didn't see her again until the NYPD float arrived. Ulysses Blackwell and the chief of police were still on the torch, waving to the crowd, and the high school police Explorers were still marching right in front of them. But there had been a small change, and Alex was the first to spot it.

"Now I've seen everything," he said, shaking his head.

It took me a second, but then I saw it too. It was Natalie, and she was marching right in the middle of the Explorers just like she was one of them. It was only then that I noticed her coat and beret were almost a perfect match for their uniforms.

The moment she got past the security guards and made it inside the restricted area, she split off from the group before anyone had a chance to notice her or question who she was.

The three of us just stood there, stunned.

"She did not just do that," Grayson said.

"Oh, she did," Alex replied. "In fact, I'm pretty sure she's going to—"

He was interrupted by Natalie's ring tone coming from the phone in his pocket.

"Give me a call and tell me all about it."

He answered the phone and listened for a moment before relaying a message: "Natalie says hello and wants everyone to know that she is okay and not in parade jail."

"Hi, Natalie," Grayson and I said into the phone, laughing.

Alex listened some more and slumped before saying, "Seriously?"

Apparently, she *was* serious, because he got down on his hands and knees, placed the phone on the ground in front of him, and bowed repeatedly toward it while saying, "I'm not worthy of you or your Omega awesomeness."

Grayson and I laughed until we had tears in our eyes. Both of us were glad that even though we'd all thought it was a bad idea, only Alex had had the nerve to tell her.

About ten minutes later, Alex's phone rang again, and Natalie told him where we could find her now that she had followed Ulysses back onto the street. When he hung up the phone, he gave me a curious look. "It was loud, and I couldn't hear her perfectly. But I think she said to tell you that we need to be careful because Ulysses is with . . . Big Red and Glass Face? Do those names mean anything to you?"

They absolutely did.

A few months earlier, Natalie and I had gone to the morgue to investigate three mysterious bodies that had been discovered on Roosevelt Island. When we got there, we were surprised to learn that the bodies were not actually dead. They were zombies, and we interrupted them right as they were trying to steal the *Book of Secrets*, which Dr. H had hidden there. Our fight with them was intense, and we barely escaped. At the time, we knew that one of the zombies was

Cornelius Blackwell, but we didn't know the other two, so we nicknamed them Big Red and Glass Face.

I explained this to the boys and told them that when we were looking through the photographs of the Unlucky 13, we had been able to identify both of them. Big Red is actually Edmund Blackwell, and Glass Face is his brother Orville.

I thought back to what we had typed out about them.

5. **Edmund Blackwell**: Deceased

   Occupation: Sandhog

   Aliases: Edmund Vanderbilt, Edmund Stanford, Edmund Flagler

   Most Recent Home: Grand Central Terminal

   Role within the 13: "the Butcher"; security for Marek

   Last Sighting: New York City Morgue/Alpha Bakery

6. **Orville Blackwell**: Deceased

   Occupation: Sandhog

   Aliases: Orville Barnard, Orville Pratt, Orville Fordham

   Most Recent Home: Hunter College

   Role within the 13: "the Enforcer"; security for Marek

   Last Sighting: New York City Morgue/Alpha Bakery

"If I remember correctly," Alex said, "aren't Edmund and Orville the ones who beat up anyone who got in Marek's way?"

"Yep," I said. "Their nicknames are the Butcher and the Enforcer."

Alex shook his head and commented, "This suddenly sounds much worse than parade jail."

We caught up to Natalie a couple of blocks away and congratulated her on her undercover work.

"Tell me one thing," I said. "Were you already planning on doing that when you picked out your coat and beret?"

She looked offended that I would even ask such a thing. "Of course I was. Have you ever seen me wear a beret before?"

Farther up the street, we saw Ulysses walking with Edmund and Orville. Orville had a serious limp, which was the result of the beat down Natalie had put on him in the morgue. She had kicked his leg so many times it almost fell completely off at the knee.

"Did one of you cause that limp?" asked Grayson.

I looked at Natalie, who smirked and said, "Maybe."

She took some pictures with her phone, and we continued to follow them from a safe distance. We now had new photos of three members of the Unlucky 13. Our work on the Baker's Dozen was off to a great start.

"Here's something I'm wondering," said Grayson. "According to the logbooks, Edmund and Orville always provided protection for Marek."

"Right," said Natalie.

"And now that he's out of the picture," he continued, "it looks like they're bodyguards for Ulysses."

"You think it's a sign that Ulysses is next in line to take charge of Dead City?" asked Alex.

Grayson nodded. "That's exactly what I think."

We followed them for about twenty minutes until they reached Grand Central Terminal. If you've never been there, trust me when I say that it's amazing. It's one of the world's largest train stations, with over forty different platforms and a massive subway station, all of which are underground.

"This is Edmund's home station," Grayson reminded us. "So I'm sure he knows every little twist and turn."

No kidding.

Unlike when they were on the street and kept things nice and leisurely, they picked up the pace once they got inside. This made it harder for us to keep up with them. So did the fact that the station was clogged with tourists who had come into the city to see the parade. I could tell they were tourists because instead of looking where they were going they kept staring up at the chandeliers and the mural of the night sky on the ceiling. At one point, I was hurrying down the grand staircase when I ran smack into someone who had stopped so that he could take a picture of the concourse.

We still managed to keep up and followed the three of them through a hidden door that led to the longest stairwell I'd ever seen. It was cut right into the bedrock, and its rusted steps seemed to descend forever. When we finally reached the bottom, we found a passageway that was part hallway and part cave. The floor was made of cement, but the walls and ceiling were jagged rock.

"Do you think this is still even part of Grand Central?" Alex whispered.

Natalie looked around and tried to get her bearings. "I'm not sure it's still part of New York," she joked while keeping equally quiet.

Since we didn't know which way the three zombies went, Natalie just picked a direction and we followed it. The hallway was curved in a way so that we couldn't see very far ahead of us, which made each step just a wee bit nerve-racking. We never knew what we might be stepping into. Finally, we reached a dead end. It was a massive steel wall with a door that seemed like it belonged on a bank vault. It was old and rusted and looked as if no one had used it in decades.

"Is it locked?" Natalie asked Alex.

He tried to open it but couldn't get it to budge.

"Either locked or rusted shut," he answered. He tried again, but this time we heard an electronic beep.

"What's that?" Alex asked, worried that he'd set off an alarm.

A hand scanner lit up on the wall. It was off to the side, so we hadn't noticed it at first, but it looked just like the ones we used to access the attic in the Flatiron Building.

"Explain this," Grayson said as he examined it. "What is something so high-tech doing down here?"

Natalie studied the door and said, "My guess is that it was installed to protect whatever's on the other side of this."

The nameplate on the door was covered in dirt and grime. Alex wiped it clean with his thumb.

"M42," he said, reading it. "Any ideas what that means?"

We all shook our heads.

"None," I said.

We poked around a little bit more, and Natalie took a picture of the nameplate and a few more of the scanner.

When we didn't find anything else that was interesting, we decided to follow the hallway in the opposite direction. Rather than a dead end, this way led us into a huge open space and a tunnel with a train platform and a single railroad car that was rotted and rusting. A faded sign on the wall read TRACK 61.

"Is this another ghost station?" I asked.

"Well, it's not a subway track," Grayson said, perplexed, as he tried to figure it out.

"And this is certainly not a subway car," Alex said as he climbed up onto its back platform.

As the rest of us walked alongside the car, Grayson reached up and rapped it with a fist. "I think it's made out of armor."

Except for the fact that it was all beat-up, it seemed like something that belonged in a museum. Natalie pointed out an official seal mounted on the side of the car.

"Check it out," she said. "Seal of the president of the United States."

"What is this place, anyway?" I asked as I bent down to tie my shoe. When I did, I looked under the train and saw some rotted wood and a rusted-out panel. And then I noticed something else on the other side.

Feet.

"We're not alone!" was all I was able to get out before the attack began.

There were five zombies in all, although at times it seemed like there were more. They worked as a team and seemed to coordinate their attacks.

The first two came running from the front of the train car and instantly engaged Natalie and Grayson. I had never seen Grayson fight before, and while he wasn't as polished as Natalie or Alex, he had some impressive skills.

I looked back to the rear platform of the train car, where a zombie had jumped Alex from behind and was now crushing him against the railing. I went to help but was caught completely off guard when a hand reached out from beneath the train and grabbed me by the ankle.

I smacked face-first into the ground, and when I turned over, I could see the zombie about to body slam me like they do in professional wrestling. I rolled out of the way just in time and whacked him in the back of the head with my cast.

It was total chaos as the fighting spread across the tunnel and platform.

The fifth and final zombie was none other than Orville Blackwell, who stood on the roof of the train car and barked orders that made no sense to us but seemed to really motivate the undead.

Despite the limp, he moved around pretty well for a guy who was over a hundred years old. At one point, he jumped off the car and landed on his feet as though it was nothing.

"Watch out!" I called over to Natalie, who was now fighting her zombie over by the tunnel wall. "I think he's looking for you."

Sure enough, Orville went straight for her, no doubt wanting revenge for what she had done to him during their fight in the morgue. When he reached her, the other zombie backed away and Orville sized her up for a moment.

Natalie was exhausted and breathing heavily, but this was still Natalie, and she was not about to show the slightest sign of weakness in front of the undead.

"Didn't you learn your lesson the last time?" she asked, trying to get a rise out of Orville. "Here, let me remind you."

She went to kick him in the same leg that she had nearly destroyed in their previous fight. But unlike before, when her foot hit his leg, he didn't crumble.

She did.

She screamed in pain as she fell to the ground and grabbed her foot. Then she looked up at Orville, and he gave her a big toothy grin as he rolled up his pant leg to reveal a thick metal pole that had replaced his damaged leg beneath the knee.

"Now you learn a lesson," he said as he bent down and lifted her by the shoulders. Natalie kicked and squirmed but couldn't break free of his grip as he slammed her against the rock wall again and again.

I felt so helpless. And then Alex came to the rescue.

He came running up from out of nowhere and in a single move managed to rip Natalie free from Orville's grasp and at the same time sucker punch him from behind with three quick jabs. Orville was dazed and turned just in time for Alex to go Krav Maga on his face. He was poking and pulling, and Orville screamed for help. The other zombies instantly stopped fighting the rest of us and rushed to help him.

At one point, it looked like Alex was going to fight all of them single-handedly, but they'd seen enough. Once they'd helped Orville to his feet, they formed a wall around him and ran into the darkness of the tunnel and disappeared.

Grayson and I did the only thing we could think of. We applauded. But Alex was in the moment, and he spun around to check on Natalie.

"Are you okay?"

Natalie was still trying to catch her breath and get up from the ground. She made it to her hands and knees but had to stop there. She looked up at Alex, and I couldn't read her expression. I was worried that she was seriously hurt until she flashed him a big smile. Then she bowed repeatedly and said, "I'm not worthy of you and your Omega awesomeness."

It was dark, so I couldn't tell for sure, but it looked like Alex was blushing.

Ω17

A Time for Giving Thanks

Do my eyes deceive me, or is my Little Molly Bear wearing makeup?"

Little Molly Bear. Ugh.

Apparently, my grandmother was under the impression that I was still four years old. Of course, I could have straightened this out by telling her that the reason I was wearing a little makeup was because I was trying to hide the cuts and bruises I'd gotten during hand-to-hand combat with a couple of killer zombies in what appeared to be an abandoned top-secret government bunker underneath Grand Central Station. But that probably would've ruined the flow of Thanksgiving dinner conversation.

And it definitely would have gotten me grounded.

So instead, I just smiled and tried to be the best Little Molly Bear I could possibly be. I passed the mashed potatoes and said, "Yes, Grandma, I wanted to look especially nice for you."

We don't have a ton of relatives, but with one set of grandparents, two aunts, an uncle, and three cousins over for Thanksgiving, we more than filled up the apartment with holiday cheer. And when it was time to hold hands and say what we were thankful for, I truly had a lot of things to choose from. There were some I listed out loud, like "great friends and an amazing family," and some I kept to myself, like "surviving this morning's run-in with the zombies and reconnecting with my undead mom."

As for dinner, we had all the Bigelow family's greatest hits. Dad made turkey and stuffing that was so good you could write poetry about them, Aunt Fiona baked not one but two of her famous Texas-style pecan pies, and Grandpa Homer ended the feast the same way he did every year, by patting his ample belly and saying, "Thanks for having us over, Michael, it's the only time I ever get a good meal."

It really was great to see my relatives again, but big family gatherings are kind of hard for me. No matter how many people are there, I still can't help noticing the hole where Mom isn't. That was especially true this year because I knew she was spending Thanksgiving all alone somewhere underneath Manhattan.

That night, after everybody left and Beth and I took care of the dishes (or, put another way: that night after everybody left and because of the cast on my hand Beth washed and dried the dishes while all I did was put them away), we found my father kicked back on the couch with a huge smile on his face and a big piece of pie on the coffee table. He was in heaven . . . but it was not going to last for long.

"What do you think you're doing?" Beth asked.

"Well, let's see," Dad said in his special Dad-pointing-out-the-obvious way. "I'm wearing my Jets jersey. I have a slice of your aunt's amazing pecan pie. And on the television, there's a football game featuring the Jets. . . . Hence the jersey. So I believe I am enjoying Thanksgiving just as the Pilgrims intended it to be enjoyed."

"Umm . . . I don't think so," she said as she picked up the remote and turned off the television. "Or have you already forgotten about family time?"

"Hey, hey, hey," Dad said as he grabbed the remote from her and turned the TV back on. "I'm pretty sure we just had family time. Don't you remember? Your grandpa patted his belly and everything."

"But you said *we* were supposed to have family time," she reminded him. "Just the three of us. Grandpas and cousins don't count. It's my turn to plan it, and I choose tonight."

Dad gave her a suspicious look as he tried to come up with a way to save his night of football. "I know," he suggested. "Why don't we watch the Jets game . . . together? That'd be fun."

"Excuse me," I interrupted. "But how is that family time?"

"I'm glad you asked," he replied, stalling as he tried to come up with an answer. "My Jets jersey . . . was a birthday present from the two of you—family. The pie was baked by your aunt Fiona—family. The TV . . . is owned by . . . you know . . . the family. Family time."

He could tell by our expressions that this was going nowhere and realized that he could not win. He took one last sad look at the game and then turned it off himself.

"Thank you," Beth said.

"My pleasure," Dad replied as though he meant it. "So what did you plan for us to do?"

"You're going to love it," she told him. "We're scrap-booking."

It was almost more than he could bear.

"Scrapbooking?" he asked, trying to make sure he heard her correctly. "You realize that I'm a very masculine member of the Fire Department of New York City, right? Scrapbook-ing's not exactly . . . my thing. Isn't there some sort of moun-tain climbing or chopping down of trees that we could do?"

"Molly," she said, turning to me. "Please remind him what he said to us."

"And I quote," I said, trying not to laugh at my dad. "'*Anything* I do with the two of you is special to me.'"

"And tonight," Beth informed him, "*anything* is scrap-booking."

She headed into her room for a moment, and Dad eyed me warily.

"I like that the two of you are working together," he said. "It would be nice if it wasn't in some evil plot to keep me from watching the Jets game, but I do like it."

To be fair, Beth wasn't just messing with Dad. There was a reason she picked scrapbooking and a reason she picked Thanksgiving night. The fact that it also messed with him was just a big bonus in her eyes. She came back out carrying a couple boxes.

"Remember when Mom kept signing us up for activities like mother-daughter yoga?"

"Or mother-daughter swing dancing," I added.

"Right, like swing dancing," she said. "Well, one time she signed us up for scrapbooking, and we started to make this."

She pulled a large scrapbook out of one of the boxes.

"The plan was that it would cover our entire family history," she said. "Except we didn't get too far before she got sick. For the longest time, I couldn't even look at it. So I just kept it under my bed."

She handed it to us, and I started flipping through it with my dad. There were about ten completed pages. They were amazing, with pictures and keepsakes from things I hadn't thought about in years. My dad ran his fingers across some old ticket stubs from a Broadway play, and I thought he was going to cry.

"I had Grandma and Grandpa Collins bring over this box of old photos from their house," she continued. "I thought tonight we could all start working on it together."

Dad was extremely quiet, and I didn't know if maybe it was all too emotional for him. But then he smiled and looked right at Beth.

"You so get what family time is all about!" Then he wrapped her up in a big bear hug.

While she was still in the hug, with her face buried in his shoulder, she decided to go for broke and mumbled, "Does that mean I get the last piece of pecan pie?"

Dad let go and stepped back. "Don't touch my pie!" he said. "I kept close count. I only had one piece. You had three."

Beth just smiled and did her little eyelash thing.

"Okay," he said, melting, "we can split it."

I cleared my throat.

"Three ways," he said, begrudgingly but not really. "We can split it three ways."

It's not an exaggeration to say it was one of the best nights of my life. We told old stories, heard a few new ones, and found some hilarious pictures of Mom and Dad when they were first dating and they looked so young.

"Notice that your mom had big hair and I had a small waist," he said with a chuckle. "Over the years those adjectives somehow managed to trade places."

By eleven o'clock, the entire floor of the living room was covered with photographs and keepsakes and none of us wanted it to end. That's when Dad went into the kitchen and started making hot open-faced turkey and stuffing sandwiches.

Not to keep using it as an excuse, but my cast made

it really hard to cut shapes and designs with those little scrapbook scissors. I had a good eye for layout, and we discovered that Dad had a knack for picking out decorations to go around the pictures and he was especially skilled at curling ribbon. (He said it was because of all his first-aid training with bandages.)

It was almost two in the morning when Dad called it quits.

"I have to get enough sleep before my shift tomorrow," he said as he got up from the floor.

"Are you going to tell your buddies in the station that you watched the football game?" Beth asked. "Or that you cut ribbon and pasted pictures all night?"

He took a deep sleepy breath as he considered the best answer.

"I'm going to tell them that I hung out with the two most beautiful, intelligent, and interesting girls in all of New York," he said as he gave us each a good-night kiss on the forehead. "And I'll tell them that we watched the Jets game together."

He headed off to bed and left Beth and me alone.

I sat there and looked at her for a moment. In some ways, Beth is so easy to underestimate. She's pretty and she's social, and you get jealous and assume that she must be shallow. But she's not. And though I'd never tell her, there are so many ways I want to be just like her.

"What are you looking at, Little Molly Bear?" she taunted.

And so many ways I don't.

"This was pretty incredible," I told her. "You know, there's no way anything I come up with for family time will be as cool."

"No, there isn't," she joked. "But I'm sure whatever you pick will be nice and weird."

"You are so very funny."

She started to clean up, and I took the box from her hand.

"Let me do this," I said. "You had to take care of the dishes. My cast won't get in the way of me picking up."

"You sure?"

"I insist."

"Okay," she said, pleased. "But be careful to keep the pictures organized. You have to put them in the right—"

"Do you want me to do it or not?" I interrupted.

She stopped herself and smiled. "Good night."

She went to her room, and I picked up. The little scraps of ribbon and paper were easy, but the pictures took a while. I couldn't just put them in the box; not only did

I have to organize them according to Beth's system, but I found myself looking at each one, reliving some moments and trying to figure out others. I was getting supersleepy, but didn't want to stop.

I was particularly excited when I found an envelope with pictures that had been taken at MIST. It was odd seeing my mom just a little bit older than me but at the same school I go to. I especially liked a photo of her with some friends on the patio. It was right next to the bench where my Omega team eats lunch every day.

Then I noticed something about the picture that woke me right up. There were two adults talking to her friends and her, and much to my surprise, I recognized both of them.

The first one was Jacob Blackwell. He was the member of the Unlucky 13 who had been killed on Halloween by being handcuffed on the subway car.

I looked at the second one and came to a realization so unexpected that I said it out loud even though I was all alone.

"I think I just found Milton Blackwell."

MIST

As I walked across Roosevelt Island from the subway station to school, I had a flashback to the first time I was there. It was the summer before sixth grade, and I'd come to the Metropolitan Institute of Science and Technology for an admissions interview. Every year, more than a thousand students from across New York City apply to MIST, and of those only about seventy-five are invited to interview for one of the openings. The biggest reason I'd applied was because it's where my mother had gone to school and I wanted to be just like her. But when I caught my first glimpse of the campus, I began to have second thoughts. It was nothing like St. Francis of Assisi, the Catholic school in Queens where I'd gone since kindergarten.

"What do you think?" asked my dad, who was walking beside me.

I stood there for a moment and studied the four gray buildings. They looked cold and ominous, and I couldn't picture ever feeling at home in them.

"I think I hate it," I answered honestly. "St. Francis looks like a school, but this looks like . . ."

". . . a really scary hospital," said a voice from behind me.

I turned around and saw a tall man with wild hair and a friendly smile. He held his hands behind his back as he leaned forward so that he could look me in the eye.

"And you know why it looks that way?" he continued. "Because that's what it was when they built it. I have come to think that buildings must have DNA just like people do, because no matter how many times we paint it or plant pretty flowers around it, the whole place still looks like something you'd see in a horror movie."

He offered me his hand and said, "I'm Dr. Gootman, the principal of this excruciatingly unattractive school."

I couldn't help but laugh. "Nice to meet you, I'm Molly Bigelow."

"That's very interesting," he said as we shook hands. "Because I am supposed to interview a prospective student named Molly Bigelow. So unless this is an amazing coincidence, I'm guessing that's you."

I nodded.

"And considering you've already told your father that you *hate* the school," he added with a humorous expression, "I'm worried that things do not bode well for the interview."

"I'm so sorry, I didn't mean to—"

He cut me off as I tried to apologize.

"There's nothing to be sorry about," he said. "It's a completely reasonable reaction. But before we go inside, I would like to ask you a question or two."

"Okay."

"What did you think the first time you saw a human heart? Not just a picture of one but an actual bloody, pulpy human heart?"

The question caught me completely off guard, and I no doubt made a doofus face as I replayed it in my head to make sure I'd heard him correctly.

"It's not what you expected me to ask, is it?"

"No," I said. "In fact, I think it's a really . . . weird question."

"It's only weird if the answer is that you've never seen one," he replied. "But you seem like someone who *has* seen a human heart before. And if that's the case, then the question might be considered . . . insightful."

And that's where he had me, because I had seen one.

"Okay, I've seen a heart before," I admitted, "but how did you know that?"

"Wouldn't it be fantastic if it was because I had some sort of extrasensory mind-reading capability?" he replied. "But, actually, I know it because in preparation for our interview I reviewed your application. In it you said your mother was a medical examiner and that you liked to help out in her office. This means the odds of you having seen one are pretty good. So I'll ask again. What did you think the first time you saw a human heart?"

This guy was not like any teacher or principal I had ever known. I glanced at my dad for a second, but he just shrugged and tried not to laugh. Then I looked back at Dr. Gootman and answered, "I thought it was really gross."

"That is also a completely reasonable reaction," he said. "In fact, if you had reacted any differently, I'd probably be concerned. But I'm curious what you thought of it when you found out that inside all those gross, disgusting parts occurs a miracle that pumps oxygenated blood throughout the body, making life possible. I want to know what you thought when you were able to look past its appearance and see it for what it truly was."

He may not have been able to read minds, but he sure seemed to know how mine worked, because I specifically remember the day when I came to the same realization and stopped being grossed out by the stuff in my mom's office.

"I thought it was beautiful."

He put his hand on my shoulder and turned me back around so that I faced the school again.

"You will find that a miracle beats inside these gross, disgusting buildings, too. It's the miracle of gifted students and talented teachers coming together. It's the miracle of education," he said. "And seven years from now, when you graduate from this school, I guarantee that you'll no longer see how it looks. You'll only see it for what it is. And I'm willing to bet that you'll think it's beautiful."

"That's . . . pretty hard to believe," I answered, not giving an inch. "But before I can do any of those things, I still have to get past my interview."

"Don't worry about that," he said as he gave me a friendly pat. "You just aced the interview."

That's how I found out that I was accepted to MIST, and nearly a year and a half later, the memory of that day brought a smile to my face as I walked onto the campus. I stopped at the same point where we'd met, and I looked at the school. While I still wouldn't call it beautiful, I had to admit that it was growing on me.

There are four main buildings on the campus, and each one is named after a letter from the Greek alphabet. Alpha is the largest and is home to the Upper School, grades nine through twelve. The Lower School, where I take most of my classes along with the rest of the sixth, seventh, and eighth graders, is in Beta. (Since it was built alongside the East River, Beta has the best daydreaming views when you get bored in class.) The cafeteria and the gym are both in Gamma, which is why the teams at MIST are nicknamed the Gamma Rays. And my favorite building is Delta because it houses most of the science labs as well as the auditorium and library.

The library is where Alex asked the rest of us to meet him during lunch that day. Apparently, my theory about the current identity of Milton Blackwell wasn't the only big revelation of Thanksgiving break. And while I wanted to do a little more research and think mine through before sharing it with the others, Alex said he had news about Track 61 and M42, the mysterious places we'd discovered underneath Grand Central Terminal. (You know it had to be important if Alex was willing to skip a meal.)

I was the last one to arrive because I had the longest walk. I found them in a back corner, away from where Ms. Turley, the media specialist, has her office.

"Can we start now?" asked Natalie, anxious to hear what he had found.

"Yes," Alex said.

He had a stack of three dusty library books that looked like they had never been checked out. He read the title of each one as he set them down on the table in front of us.

"*Techniques for Converting Electricity from AC/DC to Traction Current, Architecture of Grand Central Terminal*," he said, "and my favorite, *Secret Nazi Plots of World War II*."

"Tell me that you're not starting a book club and asking us to read these," joked Natalie. "Because I've already read *Techniques for Converting Electricity*, and I found the love story to be completely unrealistic."

"No book club," he said. "But there are a couple of things in them that I'd like to show you."

He started with the book about Grand Central. It was extremely technical and filled with complex drawings, blueprints, and schematics. It showed every detail of the train station. Or so it seemed. Alex pointed out that there was no mention of the long stairway we took or of the deep basement where we'd found M42 and Track 61.

"It's like they don't exist," he said. Then he pointed to a diagram on a different page and said, "Except both of them are listed here."

He laid it out for us to examine. I couldn't make much sense of the blueprints, but Grayson instantly understood what he meant.

"This is all wrong," he said. "They have the room and the platform on the opposite side."

"I know," Alex said. "It's a total fake out. Just like this book."

"How is the book a fake out?" I asked.

"I don't think it's real," he said. "I've searched publishing records, the Library of Congress website, the New York Public Library database; I've searched everywhere, and none of them have a record of this book ever being published."

"But you're holding it," Natalie said, "so someone must have published it."

"I think the government printed a few copies and then smuggled some into Germany during the war," he said. "I think they wanted to confuse Adolf Hitler."

This led us to the next book, *Secret Nazi Plots of World War II*. He said there was an entire chapter devoted to how the Germans wasted months planning an attack on Grand Central.

"They had two targets at the station," Alex said.

"Track 61 and M42?" asked Natalie.

"That's right," Alex answered. "Track 61 was a special platform built for the president for whenever he came to New York. It was hidden for his protection."

"And M42?" I asked.

Now he referenced the book on electricity.

"That's even better," he said. "According to this, M42 was a top-secret room built to hold the equipment that converted electricity into the right type of current to run the trains."

"Why was that such a secret?"

"Because if a Nazi spy was able to get into the room and dump just a single bag of sand into one of the converters," he explained, "it would begin a chain reaction that would stop virtually all train travel on the East Coast of the United States. During the war, trains were responsible for moving food, supplies, military troops—almost everything. To think that you could disable all of that with a bag of sand."

"It's just like crawfish jambalaya," I said, thinking about my dad's cooking lesson. "Just a little hot sauce in the perfect spot can change everything else."

"So now we know what it was," Natalie said. "But what happened to it after the war?"

"Converter technology changed," Alex said. "New equipment was installed in a different location in Grand Central, and M42 was closed for good."

"If it was shut down for good," wondered Natalie, "then when did a super-high-tech biometric palm reader get installed?"

"As for that," said Alex, "I have no idea."

"I do," answered Grayson. "It was installed a little more than six months ago."

All eyes turned to him.

"And how do you know that?" I asked.

"It occurred to me that since the undead can't leave Manhattan, they would have had to purchase it somewhere on the island," Grayson explained. "There aren't too many electronics stores that carry stuff like that, and I buy computer parts from most of them. So I had Natalie e-mail me the pictures of the scanner, and I spent Saturday taking it from store to store to see if anyone recognized it."

"And did they?" asked Alex.

Grayson nodded. "A friend at a place over in Greenwich Village."

Natalie looked excited. "I don't suppose he remembered who bought it."

"Actually, he did," Grayson said. "He said that normally

he wouldn't but that he remembered the name because it was so unusual."

He looked right at me before he continued.

"He said he sold it to a guy named Liberty."

Suddenly, everything got quiet and all eyes turned to me. Once again, I felt like I was being put in a spot to defend Liberty. I didn't know what to say.

"I told you we need to be careful about that guy," Alex said "Zombies simply cannot be trusted."

I went to defend him, but Natalie beat me to it.

"We don't know what it means," she said. "There might be a perfectly good explanation."

Alex snickered and was about to say something, but Natalie cut him off.

"I'm serious," she said. "We don't know what it means, but thanks to you guys, we know where to look. If Liberty installed it, maybe he can help us find out what it's hiding."

I think Alex would have protested more, but the bell rang. Unlike the others, who had to get to class after our lunch period ended, I had a study hall and was able to linger in the library and continue my search for the mysterious Milton Blackwell.

I found the books I was looking for in the special collections room, and since my library card had been suspended because of excessive overdue fines, I quietly slid them into my backpack and slipped out the door.

I left the library and walked along the main path that crossed the campus. As I did, I passed a row of smaller buildings that also have Greek names. Zeta is the greenhouse set up for botany class, and Sigma is the art studio. But the most interesting building in the row is known as Kappa Cottage. Originally, this was where the hospital's chief doctor lived, but now it had been converted into an office and lab for Dr. Gootman.

Dr. Gootman has an open-door policy, and I still had a little time left in my study hall and no desire to actually study, so I decided to drop in for a visit. I stepped inside and had to raise my voice so that I could be heard over the classical music playing on his old record player.

"Dr. Gootman?"

"I'm in the kitchen," he called out to me.

What had once been a kitchen now served as Dr. Gootman's own personal mini-laboratory. He was wearing his white lab coat and safety goggles as he molded a lump of clay into the shape of a volcano on the counter.

"Miss Bigelow, what a pleasant surprise," he said in that cheery voice he always had when he was working on an experiment. "Just fixing up Vesuvius here for the sixth graders."

He tossed me a pair of safety goggles, and I put them on.

"Already time for the baking soda volcano?" I asked, recognizing the project.

"It's an oldie but a goodie," he said.

"Is it as old as the music?"

"This is the *Moonlight* Sonata," he said with reverence. "A deaf man wrote this, believe it or not."

"Actually," I joked, "that's not hard to believe at all."

He leaned forward and gave me the stink eye over the top of his goggles. "Watch yourself, young lady."

I couldn't help but smile. Dr. Gootman is as much a mad scientist as he is a principal, and that's what makes him great at his job. I thought back to the first day I met him and he challenged me to see things not as they appear to be but as they truly are. It's a method I've used countless times since. And it's the method that brought me to his office that day.

I studied him for a moment and looked past the mad scientist/educator exterior and saw him for what he truly was.

I saw him as Milton Blackwell.

19

Secrets

It's easy to get distracted in the old cottage that serves as Dr. Gootman's office. It seems as though every bookshelf, cabinet, and tabletop is always overflowing with something interesting. But I was determined to keep my attention focused on him so that I could carefully read his reactions.

"To what do I owe the honor of your visit?" he asked as he continued prepping the experiment by pouring some vinegar into a beaker. "Or did you just drop by to mock Beethoven?"

"I'm having trouble with some research I'm doing and

was wondering if you could help me," I said. "Do you know anything about a man named Milton Blackwell?"

I watched his eyes for any hint of recognition, but there was none. Instead, they carefully followed the tiny droplets of red food coloring he was adding to the vinegar.

"Milton Blackwell?" He said it as though it were some foreign language. "I don't recognize the name."

I guess it would've been too easy if he'd just admitted it. After all, he'd kept his identity secret for more than a hundred years. But I knew what I knew, and I came armed with evidence. I opened my backpack and pulled out the picture that had first given me the idea. It was the one I'd found when I was putting away the old photographs of my mother.

"Maybe you'd recognize him from this picture." I held it up for him. "It was taken at MIST."

He studied the picture for a moment and shook his head.

"These goggles don't make it easy, but he's turned away from the camera too much for me to get a good look at his face." Then he added, "It's a nice picture of your mother, though."

That's when I knew I had him.

"Interesting," I said. "And how did you know she's my mother?"

Without missing a beat, he replied, "You look just like her, Molly, right down to the mismatched eyes. After all, heterochromia is genetic."

"That's true. But I think you recognized her because you're the man she's talking to in the picture. The giveaway is how he's holding his hands clasped behind his back as he leans over to look her in those mismatched eyes. You do that."

"I do?"

"Yes, you do."

"Then I guess there are at least two of us who do," he said, "because I wasn't at this school when your mother attended MIST. I've only been here for fifteen years."

"It's true that *Dr. Gootman* has only been here for fifteen years," I said. "I looked it up."

I reached into my backpack and pulled out an old yearbook that I'd taken from the library. I opened it to the faculty section and held it up for him.

"But there was a Mr. Pax who taught chemistry while my mom attended," I said. "This is him."

Once again, he gave no hint of recognition as he looked at the picture.

"He's rather ordinary-looking," he said. "Why are you showing me a photo of Mr. Pax?"

"Because he's you," I said. Then I began to hold up more yearbooks. "And so is Mr. Speranza, who taught physics in 1959, and Mr. Wissenschaft, who was selected Teacher of the Year by the class of 1940. Congratulations on that by the way. I'm sure you deserved it."

One by one, I stacked the yearbooks on the corner of a nearby table.

"The names and the subjects they teach change," I continued, "but aside from a beard here and a mustache there, the face stays the same."

Even confronted with this evidence, Dr. Gootman kept his cool and remained focused on the volcano experiment before him.

"And these pictures of average-looking men who are vaguely similar in appearance to average-looking me somehow lead you to believe that I'm Martin Birdwell?"

"Milton Blackwell," I corrected. "And, actually, the yearbook pictures only tell me that you're undead. By the way, you look great for a guy who must be pushing a hundred and forty. No, I connected you to Milton and the Unlucky 13 with the photograph of my mother."

I held it up for him again.

"The man standing next to you is your cousin Jacob, who passed away on Halloween," I explained. "I recognized him when I saw him on the news. At first, I thought it was because I'd seen his photo as one of the Unlucky 13. But when I came across this picture, I remembered that I'd also seen him here on campus . . . with you. It was about a week before he died."

This time, there was a slight flicker of reaction, a hint of sadness in his eyes.

"I'm really sorry about what happened to him," I added. "It was terrible."

He looked at me as he considered what he was going to say next.

"You need to be careful, Molly." He held a box of baking soda in one hand and the beaker of vinegar in the other. "On their own, baking powder and vinegar are harmless. But if they're mixed . . ."

He poured them both into the volcano, and within seconds, the resulting chemical reaction started spewing out of the top like lava.

". . . they can be volatile. Information is like that too. Some secrets should remain secrets."

"But if I remember the experiment correctly," I said, recalling the demonstration he'd made to my class when I was in sixth grade, "if they're mixed properly, they can help make cookies."

I pointed at the fresh batch of cookies cooling off on the opposite counter. He looked at them and then at me and smiled faintly. "And you're looking to make cookies?"

I reached over and grabbed one from the counter. "I'm certainly not trying to make a volcano."

He picked up one for himself and took a bite as he thought for a moment.

"Jacob wasn't looking to make a volcano either," he said. "That day you saw him, he'd come to warn me because he was worried about me. Protecting me is what got him killed."

He stared at the photograph for a moment, and it dawned on me that he probably didn't have many, if any, pictures of his family.

"If you'd like, you can keep that," I offered.

He looked up at me and seemed genuinely touched. "I'd like that very much."

He walked over and placed it on his desk. Then he took another bite of his cookie as his mind raced in a thousand directions.

"Milton Blackwell." He said it again, only this time he let it slowly roll off his lips. "It's been so long since anyone's called me that, I barely recognize it."

I plopped down in the comfy chair in front of his desk

and rubbed my hands together in anticipation. I had so many questions to ask him about the Unlucky 13, Marek, MIST—everything.

Then the bell rang.

"No," I moaned as I turned to the clock and saw it was time for sixth period. "This can't be. I can't go to Latin. Not now." I turned back to him. "Can you write me a pass for this period?"

"Of course I can," he said with a laugh. "But I won't."

"You won't? But . . ."

"No buts. You need to go to your class and learn Latin, and I need to make a volcano erupt for a bunch of sixth graders."

"But what about my questions?" I pleaded. "I have many, many multiple-part questions."

"I'm sure you do," he said. "But they've waited for more than a hundred years—I think they can wait until after school."

I took a deep breath and tried to compose myself.

"Okay," I said as I reluctantly got up and headed to the door. "I'll see you after school."

"Why don't you bring your friends along?"

"Really?"

"Really," he said. "But let me tell them. I'll make sure

you get the credit for the discovery, but I'd like to be the one to own up to my identity."

"It's a deal."

When I reached the door, I realized he could be pulling a fast one on me. I turned back to him and waved an accusing finger. "You will be here, right? You promise you won't try to get away?"

"You can trust me," he promised. "I'll be here."

The Unwanted

H e wasn't there.

I was standing outside Kappa Cottage, cupping my hands over my eyes so that I could look through the window by the door, and there was no sign of anyone— living or undead—inside. Every light was off. Every door was locked. Dr. Gootman had lied to me. I'd uncovered his true identity, and he'd made a run for it.

"I do not believe it," I said, furiously rattling the door-knob to no avail. "I do not believe he isn't here."

"Wow," Alex joked at my expense. "This really is the biggest surprise of the year. Dr. Gootman's door . . . has a lock."

"I never knew that!" Grayson added with mock amazement. "Do you think it's a dead bolt?"

Okay, not only had Dr. Gootman lied to me, but he was making me look stupid in front of my friends. I had texted them to meet me after school at the cottage for an "earth-shattering" surprise. This was supposed to be my moment.

"You don't understand," I said, my frustration level rising. "You just . . . don't . . . understand." I looked back through the window and tried the doorknob again.

"Sure, I understand," Alex said, needling me some more. "You're a little jealous because I found out all the information about M42 and Track 61, and Grayson figured out that Liberty installed the hand scanner, so you wanted to . . ."

"Dr. Gootman is Milton Blackwell."

I couldn't stop myself. I just blurted it out. Actually, I blurted it so fast it was probably more like "Dr.Gootman-isMiltonBlackwell." But you get the point. And, yes, I remember I had promised to let him tell them, but he'd promised not to run away so I figured that deal was off.

"What?" Natalie said in total disbelief, trying to compute it all in her head. "Dr. Gootman?"

Grayson and Alex exchanged stunned looks and then

turned back to me. It was around this time that I realized a school courtyard filled with students was probably not the best place to announce that the principal was living under a false identity. But the genie was already out of the bottle, and I could tell by their expressions that the others wanted to make sure they'd heard me right.

"Dr. Gootman is Milton Blackwell," I said again, but this time slowly and in a whisper only loud enough for the three of them to hear.

"Well, so much for letting me tell them," a perturbed voice responded.

I looked up and quickly had to amend two of my assumptions. First of all, my whisper was apparently loud enough for at least four people to hear. And since the fourth was Dr. Gootman, my runaway pronouncement may have been a bit premature.

"I'm so sorry," I said lamely. "But the door was locked, and I figured that meant you'd . . . you know . . . become a fugitive."

"Really? *Fugitive* was the most likely explanation?" he asked as he nodded down to the large volcano model that filled his arms. "Not that I'd locked up because I'd gone to Beta to do the volcano demonstration for the sixth graders?"

"Well, now that you say it," I responded, "that's also a logical explanation."

I was completely frustrated with myself, and not just because I'd been so impatient. It was mostly because I knew that it probably did have something to do with me being jealous of the boys and wanting to one-up them as quickly as I could.

"Is it true, Dr. Gootman?" Natalie asked him softly. "You're Milton Blackwell?"

He forced a smile and nodded. "Yes. It's true."

We helped him carry the volcano experiment into the cottage, and despite his initial frustration, he didn't seem too mad at me for telling the others. First, we sat around his conference table and he had me show the others my yearbook evidence. Humbled by my earlier mistakes, I toned down my self-congratulatory tone and kept it pretty straightforward. When I was done, Dr. Gootman took over.

"It really is impressive," he said. "Molly is only the third person to ever figure this out."

Okay, I'll be honest. I had assumed I was the first. Humility lesson number two. But it did make me wonder something. "Was one of the others . . . ?"

"Yes," he said before I could finish. "One of the others

was your mother. Apparently, Sherlock Holmesian skills of deduction are just as genetic as heterochromatic eyes."

"If two others figured it out, then how come there's no mention of it in the Baker's Dozen files?" asked Natalie.

"Because those teams did what I am going to ask you to do," he said. "They kept it a secret. They didn't leave any evidence anywhere. Not even with a manual typewriter at the top of the Flatiron Building."

"Why do you need it to be a secret?" Grayson asked. "Because it puts you in danger?"

"No, if it was just me, it wouldn't be such a big deal," he explained. "But the simple truth is that to many of the citizens of Dead City, I am to blame for their condition because I built the explosive that started it all. If word ever got out that I was here, a never-ending stream of Level 2s and 3s would come to MIST looking for revenge. And that would endanger all my students, which is something I cannot let happen. I understand if you feel you can't keep this secret. I do, however, ask that if you're going to share it, you first give me a few days to make arrangements so that I can disappear properly."

"Wait a second," Alex said. "You can't *disappear*. You run the school. You make everything possible."

"That's kind of you to say, but hardly true," he replied.

"Just as Newton's First Law of Motion says of momentum, this school will continue to move in a straight line unless compelled to change that state. There were gaps of five to ten years before the arrivals of Mr. Pax, Mr. Speranza, and Mr. Wissenschaft. The school continued to prosper in my absence in those periods, and it will do so when Dr. Gootman suddenly retires, whether that's in two days or two years."

"But where would you go?" I wondered.

"I'm afraid that is something I cannot share."

"You don't have to worry," I said. "Your secret's safe with us."

"Really?" he said, only half joking. "'Cause you didn't do such a good job keeping it earlier."

I was so embarrassed with myself.

"Really," I said. "That was a one-time-only malfunction."

He looked around the table at the others. "You all feel the same?"

The others nodded and smiled.

"We won't write or mention a thing," Grayson promised.

"Okay, then," he said. "I'll make some popcorn. This could take a while."

First, he showed us some clips from some videotapes he was making that chronicled the entire history of the Blackwells and what happened before and after the subway tunnel explosion. Then he suggested we go for a walk around the island that had been his home for more than a century.

A pathway wraps around Roosevelt Island like a ribbon, and together the five of us walked along it as Dr. Gootman told us about the Unlucky 13. We discussed the explosion in the subway tunnel and the three wise men who had banished them to the dungeon at the Asylum. He also answered some of our nagging questions.

"Why do some people become undead when they die while others do not?" I asked.

"I only know of two ways to become undead," he answered. "It happens if you die a sudden death surrounded by Manhattan schist, which is what happened to the thirteen of us in the tunnel. And it happens if you get infected by exposure to the undead, which is what happened to your friend Liberty."

We stopped walking for a moment when we reached the Blackwell House. It was now a museum, but back in 1896, it still belonged to his family. This was where he had his final confrontation with his brother Marek.

"I had to make a choice," he explained. "I could have gone along with Marek and let him kill our grandfather, or I could have defied him and in the process cut myself off from my brothers and cousins."

"Do you think it was the right choice?" asked Alex.

"I know it was," he said with certainty. Then he looked at the house for a moment and added, "Although it was a very lonely choice, and there are moments of weakness when I wonder how things would have turned out if I'd chosen otherwise."

"And you stayed on the island after that?" Natalie asked.

"I thought I would be safe here. I knew that Marek would never want to come back to this place he liked to call a 'godforsaken island.' In 1896, this was home to the Asylum, the prison, and a smallpox hospital. There were a few scattered homes like my grandfather's, but mostly this was where New York sent its unwanteds. Among those were the children in the smallpox hospital. No teachers would risk going in there for fear that they would catch the disease and die."

Grayson turned to him and smiled. "But you couldn't die."

"That's right," he said. "So I began to teach at the hospital. And I was happy. I thought that it was my calling to help those sick children. But then I started to hear stories about monsters in Manhattan. People with unexplained powers who lived underground and could withstand bullets. Some people claimed they were werewolves or vampires. But I knew it was Marek and the others. And since I couldn't stop them by myself, I decided to train others who could."

Natalie stopped walking and turned to him. "The Omegas? You started the Omegas?"

"Well, first I had to start MIST," he said. "But, yes, I started the Omegas to fix the problems I had created."

Our walk had brought us back to the campus. Knowing what I now knew made it look a little different.

"But how did you just *start* a school?" Alex asked, motioning to the campus full of buildings.

"Fortunately, I wasn't the only one with a guilty conscience. My grandfather owned much of the property on the island. He also owned a construction company. He made much of this possible. And then there was one of the three wise men."

I turned to him. "Theodore Roosevelt?!"

Dr. Gootman laughed. "Quite the interesting fellow."

I got goose bumps when I thought about the idea of Dr. Gootman actually knowing Teddy Roosevelt.

"He helped you?" asked Grayson.

"Very much," he said. "It's amazing what you can accomplish if you have help from the president of the United States."

We were now at the door to the cottage.

"I have one last question," I said. "Actually, I have hundreds of questions, but one last one I want to ask you now."

"What is it?"

"Why did Jacob come to warn you? What had changed things?"

He thought about it for a moment and looked out over the campus to the East River.

"You did, Molly."

"Me? How did I change things?"

"You beat Marek. And when he fell from the top of the George Washington Bridge, everything changed. Ever since our escape back in 1896, Marek has told the others what to do. With him out of the picture, they will all try to take control of Dead City."

"I'm so sorry," I said.

"Don't be," he replied. "Marek came looking for you because he knew you were strong enough to beat him. He thought he could get to you while you were young. But you were already too strong. And so was your team."

He looked at the four of us and shook his head with wonder.

"You four are amazing," he said, giving us quite the morale boost. "Don't ever be sorry for that. You're the reason I created the Omegas. I hoped that one day it would produce people like you. Because, believe me, we're going to need them."

Ω21

Blue Moon

Amazing or not, we were running out of time and needed help. There was less than a month until Marek's Verify on New Year's Eve, and all we knew for sure was that once the crystal ball dropped to signal a new year, someone was going to take control of Dead City. Beyond that we had no idea what was going to happen.

We thought there might be some answers hidden deep below Grand Central Terminal in M42, so we went looking for Liberty. He'd installed the security system, and we hoped he could help us get inside.

Since we'd had a few too many close calls crashing flat-line parties, we decided to try a different method of contacting him this time. We went to the farmer's market in Union Square, where he told us he met his mother every Saturday. Unlike the flatline parties, there was less danger and more snacks. Yum.

"I'm going to go on the record and say that kettle corn is the greatest invention of all time," I proclaimed as I stuffed a fistful of it into my mouth and crunched.

"Even more than, say . . . the computer . . . or the Internet?" offered Grayson.

"Both great inventions," I mumbled as I tried to talk and chew at the same time. "But kettle corn is sweet *and* salty. It's easy to carry, and unlike computers and the Internet . . . it's delicious."

"She makes a compelling argument," Alex added as he reached into my bag and stole a handful for himself.

It was a cool December morning, and we were walking around eating snacks because Alex insisted we watch Liberty from a distance and approach him after his mother left.

"He only has family one morning a week," Alex explained. "Let's not take that from him."

(You see, deep down Alex has a huge heart.)

Liberty's mom left around noon, and we caught up with him in front of a booth where a man was selling homemade pretzels.

"I saw you the second you arrived," Liberty said, shaking his head. "I hope you guys do a better job hiding when you're following the bad guys."

"We weren't trying to hide from you," Natalie said, "just your mom."

He considered this for a moment and smiled. "Thanks for that. I appreciate it."

When we told him about M42, he wasn't impressed.

"*That's* why you came looking for me?" he asked. "Because you found a secret room from World War II?"

"Well, we were hoping you'd tell us what's inside it now," Natalie said.

Liberty seemed totally confused. "How would I know that?"

"Didn't you install the biometric hand scanner that controls the door?" Alex said.

"No . . . although, now that you mention it, I do remember setting one up for Winston. But I don't know where he installed it. I gave it to him in his office."

I knew from our research into the Unlucky 13 that Winston Blackwell was in charge of the portion of Dead

City directly beneath us. His home station was Union Square, and he was Liberty's stationmaster.

7. **Winston Blackwell**: Deceased

   Occupation: Businessman

   Aliases: Winston Grant, Winston McClellan, Winston Burnside

   Most Recent Home: Union Square

   Role within the 13: Organization and Logistics

   Last Sighting: Greenwich Village

"If you didn't know anything about it," Alex said, somewhat suspicious, "why did he ask you to set it up for him?"

"Like I told you guys before. Every now and then I do some computer work for them, and in exchange, I get to give my little speeches and move around Dead City without getting hassled too much," he answered. "It was just one of those times. There was nothing special about it. Winston told me that he was going to take care of the installation. He just needed me to buy a new scanner and fix it."

"If it was new," I wondered aloud, "why did it need to be fixed?"

"Palm scanners measure all the different aspects of your

hand and turn them into a geometric equation," he explained. "They're great for security . . . unless you're undead."

"Why?" I asked.

"Body heat," Grayson said, figuring out the problem. "They're triggered by body heat."

"That's exactly right. I had to reprogram the scanner so that it would recognize hands like mine," he said, wiggling his fingers for emphasis. "Winston also had me create security profiles for the whole group."

"What group?" asked Natalie.

"The Unlucky 13," he said. "They get pretty secretive about who's doing what with whom. So Winston had me build a separate profile for each one of them. That way, I wouldn't know who it was really for. All he had to do was bring it to the ones he wanted and scan their palms into the profiles I'd built."

We mulled this over for a moment.

"So the only way to open the door to M42 is to have one of the Unlucky 13 with you," Natalie said. "That should be . . . impossible."

She looked defeated, but Grayson smiled as he had a brainstorm. "Wait a second," he said excitedly. "You don't technically need one of them. You only need one of their hands."

"Okay, ewwww," said Natalie. "I'm not sure where you're going with this, but let me stress, ewwww."

"Jacob Blackwell was one of the Unlucky 13 before he was killed on the subway," he pointed out. "Can't we dig him up and get his hand?"

Natalie shook her head. "You're kind of freaking me out, Grayson. I don't expect stuff like this from you—Alex maybe, but not you."

"Hey, what's that supposed to mean?" Alex protested.

"You know what it means," Natalie said. "It means . . ."

Before this could escalate into an argument, Liberty jumped back into the conversation. "You know, there is an easier way that doesn't require any grave robbing or dismemberment."

Suddenly, everybody stopped talking, and all eyes turned to him.

"You remember the part where I said I programmed it to recognize hands like mine?" He held his hand up and wiggled his fingers again. "I did that by actually programming it to recognize my hand."

Natalie looked at his hand and smiled. "I like this plan better," she said. "No ewwww."

Thirty minutes later, we were at Grand Central, walking down the seemingly endless series of stairwells that according to the blueprints did not exist. Along the way, we told Liberty all about our last visit, when Orville Blackwell and his thugs attacked us at the hidden train platform.

"You survived an attack from Orville?" he asked Natalie, obviously impressed. "Not many people can say that. You know, there's a reason they call him the Enforcer down here."

"Well, I don't know if there is much to brag about. He pretty much redecorated the wall with my body," she replied while she rubbed a sore spot on the back of her head. "Luckily, Alex was there to rescue me."

"I guess we have that in common," Liberty said, "because I can say the same thing about Alex being there to rescue me in Morningside Park."

"Our hero," Natalie said.

"Yes, he definitely is our hero," Liberty added.

"Can we focus here?" Alex asked, embarrassed by the praise. "Or I might not save you next time."

When we reached the bottom, Liberty ran his fingers along the jagged rock that made up the walls of the hallway. "You weren't kidding when you said it was creepy down here."

"That's saying something coming from a guy who spends a good bit of his time in Dead City," Grayson said with a laugh.

We started walking along the curved hallway toward M42, and with memories of the Orville ambush still fresh in our minds, we did our best to keep quiet and stay alert. At one point, we stopped cold when we heard a noise just around the curve heading our way. It was too close for us to retreat, so we got into fighting positions. The noise got closer and closer until we finally saw our enemy . . . a giant rat scurrying along the wall. We each breathed a sigh of relief. (Okay, so Liberty didn't actually "breathe" in the classic sense, but you get my meaning.)

"I don't know about you guys," I said, "but it's a little troubling that we've reached a point in our lives when coming across a hideously large sewer rat is a reason to be relieved."

The others laughed, and we continued until we got to the door.

"Don't touch the scanner," Liberty instructed us as he moved to the front of the group to examine it. He squatted down and looked at it as closely as he could without making contact.

"This is definitely the one I set up for Winston," he said quietly. "And the good news is that it doesn't look like it's been used in the last twelve hours."

He stood up and now used his regular speaking voice.

"Hopefully, that means that there isn't anyone inside there."

"How can you tell that?" asked Grayson.

"It's in a deep sleep mode to save battery power," he replied. "If it had been used more recently than that, there'd still be a little red light blinking on and off."

"All right, then," Natalie said with a sly smile. "Let's take a look inside."

Liberty pressed his palm against the scanner, and a green laser instantly began tracing the outline of his hand. After a few seconds, we heard a loud click come from inside the door.

"We're in," Liberty said with a touch of evil genius to his voice.

Alex opened the door to reveal a massive room. There were hard metal edges and old-school electronics everywhere you looked. I'm sure when they built it, everything seemed modern and futuristic, but now it just looked like an outdated museum exhibit about early computers. The floor was a combination of cement and metal grates, while endless ducts of wiring ran along the ceiling.

"Should we be concerned that the lights are already on?" I whispered nervously.

Natalie nodded. "I know I am," she replied. "Let's make sure we're alone."

It was all much bigger than I'd expected. In addition to the main room, there were doorways to several other rooms along the far wall, and a hallway that disappeared into darkness. We silently poked around until we were satisfied that no one else was there.

"Is it just me, or does this place look like it's from one of those old spy movies?" Grayson asked. "You know, like when James Bond makes it into the supervillain's master control room?"

"That's exactly what I was thinking," Liberty answered. "I thought I knew a lot about computers, but I don't recognize any of these electronics."

"These are the converters that turned the electricity into traction current for the trains," Alex said, pointing toward a bank of tall gray machines with big dials and gauges. "They worked with these turbines." He gestured toward a row of massive fans that ran down the middle of the room.

"I don't think the Unlucky 13 are coming down here to convert electricity to run trains," Natalie said. "So let's look around and see if we can figure out why this place was worth adding the high-tech security."

We started snooping around, and I came across an old metal cabinet and managed to wiggle its door open.

Everything inside of it was covered in a thick layer of dust. There were office supplies, like pens and paper clips, which I expected, but there was also a calendar that seemed out of place.

I called over to Alex, who was checking out one of the turbines. "You said this was closed right after World War II, right?"

"In 1946, according to the book," answered Alex.

"Then why do they have a calendar from 1967?" I asked.

I held up the calendar for him to see.

Alex just shrugged. "That makes no sense to me."

"Hey," Grayson said as he stepped out of an office. "I think you guys might want to check this out."

We hurried over, and when we reached the room, it was obvious why he'd called us. It looked like it had been decorated by a demolition team. Everything was either bent or broken. There was a metal desk and three filing cabinets. Each drawer had been pried open, and there were broken padlocks scattered on the floor.

"Did you do this?" Natalie jokingly asked Grayson.

"Yes," he deadpanned. "I broke all of these thick metal locks with the superhuman strength I've been hiding from you the last few years."

Alex looked closely at one of the file cabinets and shook

his head in disbelief. "Whoever did this was strong, and I mean really strong," he said. "It looks like it was broken off with a sledgehammer. It's a clean break, which means it only took a couple hits at most."

"Well, I'm guessing that whatever they wanted was in here," Natalie said.

"Did you use your superdetective Spidey sense to come up with that?" Alex joked.

"Let's just figure out what these files are," she said.

I couldn't help but think it was a lot like when we started on the Baker's Dozen and went into the attic of the Flatiron Building for the first time. Once again we were digging through old file cabinets. What we found inside them began to paint a picture of M42 and what took place there.

Apparently, the fact that M42 was so far underground and secret made it too valuable to the government for it to just go to waste. When it was no longer needed to convert electricity for the trains at Grand Central, it was turned into a top-secret shelter for government spies. Immediately following World War II, the US government was worried about communists trying to infiltrate or attack New York City. M42 was repurposed to make sure that didn't happen.

"Listen to this," Alex said, reading from one file. "In case of an emergency, the agents were supposed to come here, where they could survive for up to three months. It can be completely sealed off from the outside world and has a kitchen, a communication center, and down the hall there's supposed to be a medical center with an operating room."

"What type of emergency were they worried about?" Natalie wondered.

"All sorts of them, going by what I've got over here," Grayson said from behind a stack of files. "These are all different plots or strategies that the government was worried the Russians might use."

"Do you think the Unlucky 13 might try one of them now?" I asked.

"I don't see how," he said. "They all seem useless."

"Why?" asked Alex.

"Most of them rely on technology that no longer exists," he said. "Like this one called 'Operation Alexander Graham Bell.'"

He held up a file folder.

"It explains how the Russians could knock out communication by disabling the switchboards at all the major office buildings in town, but nobody uses phones like that anymore. Cell phones are completely different."

He picked up another file.

"Or this one, which wonders how many communists you would need in New York City before it began to change public opinion in favor of the Soviet Union." He looked up at the rest of us. "The Soviet Union fell apart decades ago."

Something written on the cover of that file, however, caught Liberty's attention. "Wait a second," he said, turning his head to try to read it. "What's the name of that one?"

"Well, it was originally called 'Operation Red Tide,'" Grayson said. "But someone changed the name to 'Operation Blue Moon.'"

Liberty considered this for a moment.

"That's it," he said, suddenly anxious. "Blue Moon is why they put the scanner on the door. Read the first page."

Grayson didn't see the point, but Liberty was adamant, so he went along with it and started to read the report out loud. "'Although there is widespread distrust of the Soviet Union throughout the country, social scientists predict that if as few as ten to fifteen percent of the people in a big city such as New York were to change their opinion, it could start a ripple effect that would eventually grow into a majority.'"

Grayson looked right at Liberty.

"It's not going to happen," he said. "The Soviet Union doesn't even exist anymore. And if it did, ten to fifteen percent of the population of New York is about a million people. You can't turn a million New Yorkers into communists."

Liberty had a panicked look on his face, and it dawned on me why.

"No," I said, suddenly short of breath, "but maybe you could turn them into zombies."

Ω 22

Scars

A million people turned into zombies. Just the thought of it sent a chill up my spine. I sat there for a moment contemplating the mass zombiefication of New York City when it dawned on me that I'd used the z-word in front of Liberty.

"I'm so sorry," I apologized. "I should never have said that."

"It's okay," he told me. "It's a terrifying thought, no matter what word you use."

Natalie considered it for a moment and asked, "Do you really think it's possible? Do you really think they could make a million people undead?"

"No way," Alex answered.

"Maybe not," agreed Liberty. "But that doesn't mean they wouldn't try to turn as many as they could. How many undead in New York would it take for acceptance to begin? That's what they're after most of all. Ever since the three wise men sentenced them to the dungeon, the undead have been looking to come up from the underground and gain acceptance among the living. They call it the Rise of the Undead."

And there goes another chill up my spine.

Grayson reached the end of the file and handed it to Natalie. "I don't know if this is important or not, but the last couple pages have been ripped out. The conclusions are missing."

"And by 'conclusions,' you mean . . . ?"

". . . all the ways the government came up with to stop the plan," he answered.

"Too bad," Natalie replied. "Those might have been helpful."

"Suddenly, this is sounding kind of ominous," I said.

Natalie looked at the torn pages in the back of the file, and then she turned to the cover, where someone had crossed out the original name and written in a new one. "What's significant about Blue Moon? What does it mean?"

"It's just an astronomical phenomenon," answered Grayson. "It refers to the second full moon of a calendar month."

"Or it can be a saying," I added. "Something that's rare only happens 'once in a blue moon.'"

Natalie shook her head and looked right at Liberty. "But it means something different to you, doesn't it? The instant you heard it, you were convinced that the Unlucky 13 were involved. Why?"

He hesitated for a moment, unsure whether or not he should share something with us. Then he took off his jacket, revealing a T-shirt with a Columbia University logo on it. He paused again and then pulled up his right sleeve.

"This is what 'blue moon' means to the undead." On his shoulder, there was a purplish blue scar about the size of a nickel and in the shape of a crescent moon.

"How'd you get that?" I asked.

He shook his head. "Nobody knows where it comes from. All we know is that everybody who's undead has one."

"Everyone?" I asked.

He nodded, and for the first time since I'd met him, Liberty seemed vulnerable. He quickly covered it up and put his jacket back on. We were all quiet for a moment as we considered what we'd discovered.

The thought that the undead might be planning something like Operation Blue Moon was chilling, but what we found next literally gave me nightmares. We ventured farther down the hall and came across the operating room that had been set up to care for the spies in case of an attack.

"Not exactly state-of-the-art," said Grayson as we surveyed the contents of the room. There was a rusty old examination table and medical equipment that was so outdated, it looked more like something you'd find in a horror movie than in a hospital. But in the corner of the room, there were two modern additions—a small refrigerator and a long freezer. Both were plugged in and we could hear their motors whirring.

Even though we all wondered what was inside them, none of us made a move to open either one. After a few moments, Natalie stepped forward. "Fine," she said. "Don't everyone be in such a rush to be brave."

I cringed as she reached for the refrigerator. She took a deep breath and opened the door to reveal three shelves of plastic bags like the ones doctors use to hold blood for transfusions. Only these didn't have blood in them. Natalie reached in and pulled one out. She held it up to the light of the refrigerator, and we could see that it held some sort of green goop. She offered it to Liberty.

"Know what this is?"

"We call it zombie juice," he answered as he took it from her.

"Hey, watch the z-word," I joked.

"I can say it," he answered with a smile. "You can't."

He examined the bag for a moment and added, "I've never seen it stored like this."

She put it back in the refrigerator and closed the door. Next she moved over to the freezer and put her hand on the lid.

"Call me crazy, but I have a feeling we're not going to like what we see in here."

(We'll call this an understatement.)

The instant she lifted the lid the light from inside the freezer flooded the room. It was closely followed by a hideous odor I recognized from my many days at the morgue. When I'm there, I also carry vanilla to fight the smell. . . . Unfortunately, I didn't have any on me now.

Natalie fought back the gag reflex and took a look inside. She leaned over and started to list off the contents. "Let's see. One arm, one lower leg, and a hand."

"Don't forget the finger," Liberty said, pointing into the freezer.

"Sorry about that," she said. "And one finger."

I stepped closer and peeked in. For some reason, this all seemed more upsetting than anything I'd seen in the morgue. Everything there felt hygienic and scientific. Here it was just gross. It didn't help to see the body parts resting in a mixture of ice and rock. I reached in and pulled out a piece of it.

"Manhattan schist?" I asked.

Liberty nodded.

Unlike Natalie and me, the boys didn't have morgue experience, and they were turning green.

"You wanna shut that?" Alex suggested.

Natalie started to close the lid, but I reached over to stop her.

"Wait," I said. "Check the shoulder."

She gave me a confused look for a second and then smiled when she realized what I meant. She bent over to get a close look at the shoulder.

"Yep," she said. "Blue moon."

"So we know that it belonged to someone who was already undead."

"Seriously," Grayson said, trying to talk and hold his breath at the same time. "Can you please shut that?"

Natalie let the lid fall shut with a thud. She was just about to make a joke when we heard a noise. Someone was activating the scanner to open the main door to M42.

In a flash, Natalie took charge and motioned us to follow her two doors down, where there was an empty office. We slipped inside and shut the door so that it was barely cracked open.

We heard the main door open and shut, followed by the noise of a squeaky wheel turning again and again. It reminded me of someone pushing an old shopping cart. We weren't sure how many people were out there, but we could hear at least two talking.

"You left the lights on again," the first voice said.

The second voice replied in the broken English that some of the undead use. It didn't make sense to me, but it must have to the first guy, because he laughed.

"If everyone knew how scared you are of the dark, they'd stop calling you the Enforcer."

Orville.

Orville was the Enforcer, and knowing he was out there made me try that much harder to remain perfectly still. We could only see a small sliver of the hall through the crack in the doorway, and when they walked past, we could see that the other person was Edmund. As if we hadn't already had enough fun with Big Red and Glass Face.

Luckily, they were too busy to notice us. They were

pushing an old hospital bed loaded with supplies that, unlike the ones in the room, were brand-new. Just enough light came in for me to see the worried expression on Natalie's face.

My pulse was racing, and it felt like my heart was beating all the way up in my throat. They wheeled the bed into the operating room, and the instant we heard the door slam shut behind them, Natalie bolted into action.

"Let's go now!" she said more as a command than a suggestion.

"What about them?" Alex asked. "Orville? Edmund? The operating room? Shouldn't we see what they're doing?"

She was determined. "No way! We're getting out of here before anyone else arrives."

She poked her head out the doorway and made sure everything was clear, then she motioned for all of us to follow her. We moved as quickly and quietly as possible down the hall and through M42, toward the main door.

"Can't we just go take a peek?" Alex asked, not giving up.

"The space is too confined," she said. "We'll get caught."

Alex shrugged. "So what? There are five of us and two of them. I like our odds."

"First of all, there are four of us," she said. "We've already asked a lot of Liberty to help us this far. He's a part of Dead City, and we can't ask him to fight the Unlucky 13. And second, we don't know how many more are on their way."

Alex was frustrated and went to say something, but she didn't want to hear it. She just cut him off and said, "This is not a debate. I'm in charge, and we're leaving. Now!"

I'd never seen the two of them so much at odds with each other. And I'd have to say it wasn't the ideal location for this to happen. Still, Natalie was not backing down, and after a few deep breaths, Alex relented. The mood stayed pretty tense as we snuck out of the shelter and then during the long climb back up the stairs. No one really talked until we reached Grand Central, where all the arms and legs we saw were actually attached to living, breathing people.

"Can I talk now without you pulling rank on me?" Alex asked, more than a little peeved.

"Sure," Nat snapped back at him.

"I don't understand what happened down there," he complained. "The Unlucky 13 is setting up a secret operating room a couple hundred feet underground. There are mysterious body parts in a freezer. There are new medical supplies being brought in. That sounds exactly like the kind of thing that we should investigate."

Natalie thought for a moment before responding, and I couldn't tell if she was regretting her decision or was just angry at Alex. Maybe it was both.

"I didn't think it was safe," she said. "There was only one door in and out of there, and we had no idea how many people were coming behind them. There was too much of a chance that we'd get trapped."

"What happened to Danger Girl?" he said, shaking his head in disbelief. "Normally, I'm the one trying to get you to be more careful. Didn't you risk getting arrested by marching in the Thanksgiving Day Parade just to sneak up to Ulysses Blackwell?"

"I did," she said, her voice rising. "And do you remember how that day turned out? I got slammed against a rock wall a couple times. Maybe it knocked some sense into me, because I will not let that happen to anyone else."

Suddenly, it made sense why she was being more cautious than usual.

"I'm sorry," Alex said. "I should have been more sensitive to that."

"It's okay," she replied, her mood calming down. "I just want us to be careful."

"I want that too," he said softly. "You made the right call."

There was an awkward silence, and I decided to break the tension, or at least try to, with a little humor. Not always my strong suit, but I'm getting better.

"Are we done fighting? Because I haven't had anything to eat since that kettle corn, and it's making me cranky. Oh, and so is the thought that the Unlucky 13 might be planning to unleash the zombie apocalypse on Manhattan."

"There's that word again," kidded Liberty. "Remember, I can say it and you can't."

"I'm so sorry," I said. "Do you guys see what the hunger is doing to me? It's making me insensitive."

Luckily, there was a cinnamon pretzel stand nearby, and I was able to calm the rumbling in my stomach long enough for us to say our farewells. Mostly, I wanted to make sure that Alex and Natalie were all patched up and that Liberty knew how much we appreciated his help.

"I promise we won't keep popping up unannounced," Natalie said to him.

"Good," he said. "But I'm more worried about Blue Moon. What are you all going to do about it? You're on the Baker's Dozen. You've got to take charge."

"The problem is that we don't really know what it is," Natalie responded. She turned to Grayson. "Any chance your big old computer can find a copy of that file without the final pages ripped out?"

Grayson smiled. "If it's out there, Zeus can find it."

"Zeus?" Liberty said, confused.

"He thinks his computer's a person," Nat explained.

Grayson went to deny this, but then stopped himself. "I kind of do."

We all laughed, and that helped improve the mood.

"I'll start him searching tonight," he continued. "But CIA documents are usually encrypted, so it could take a while for him to find what we're looking for."

"Don't take too long," Liberty said as we were about to leave. "I've been thinking about Marek missing his Verify. That's going to be huge. And it's going to happen at midnight on New Year's Eve, when a million people come to Times Square."

"A million people," I said, making the connection. "Sounds like the perfect time to try out Operation Blue Moon."

Ω23

Time Management

One of the real drawbacks of being an Omega is that in addition to finding random body parts and uncovering plots for the zombie apocalypse, you also have to make time for regular life stuff like doing chores and finishing your homework. I caught a break (literally) when I fractured my hand and got out of some chores for six weeks. But the day the doctor removed my cast (or as my sister liked to call it, "the neon purple excuse machine"), Beth greeted me at the front door with a sponge and a dish towel and simply said, "You're it." Apparently, I'm now on dish duty for the rest of my life.

As far as homework goes, I returned from our terrifying adventure into M42 and was still coping with the above-mentioned "parts and plots" when I got another shocker. I glanced in my planner and realized that I had only one day to cram for a major math test, build a shoebox diorama of Edgar Allan Poe's "The Tell-Tale Heart," and write a three-page research paper about the War of 1812.

The last thing I needed was a couple of bad grades just as winter break was about to begin. Nothing says "home for the holidays" quite like being grounded the week of Christmas and New Year's. So I woke up Sunday morning determined to focus on nothing but schoolwork.

I started off by creating special playlists designed to provide the perfect mood music as I worked on each one of my assignments. Sure, this took a little while, but I was certain it would come in handy down the line.

Next, in order to relax both physically and mentally, I walked over to Astoria Park and shot baskets until I was able to make ten free throws in a row. This way I knew my mind and body were in perfect harmony with each other and therefore in the ideal state to do my best work.

Finally, I headed over to Grayson's to hang out . . . I mean, I headed over to Grayson's to use his computer for help on my research paper. Zeus really is the most amazing computer I've ever seen, and the fact that Grayson pretty much built it from scratch gives you an idea of how talented he is. The fact that after an hour of using it, I'd only written a paragraph and a half of my term paper gives you an idea of how disinterested I was in doing homework.

Everything made my mind wander. I was reading about the British Army invading Washington, DC, but I could only think about the undead invading New York. I was trying to compose the perfect topic sentence when I got distracted by an amazing aroma.

"What is that?" I asked. "It smells delicious."

"Latkes."

I crinkled up my nose as I tried to figure out what a latke was. "What are they?"

"Potato pancakes," he said. "My mom makes them every year for the first day of Hanukkah. They're delicious."

Grayson's family is Jewish, it was the first day of Hanukkah, and I was in the way. How very Molly of me.

"I'm sorry," I said. "Am I interrupting some special family time?"

"That's not until dinner," Grayson said. "How's your paper coming along?"

I looked up at him and smiled sheepishly. "Can't we just talk about the latkes and forget the paper?"

"That bad, huh?"

"I'm just having trouble building enthusiasm for the War of 1812," I answered. "It seems kind of insignificant in light of the impending zombie apocalypse scheduled for New Year's Eve. Speaking of which, has Zeus had any success in his search for the missing pages of Operation Blue Moon?"

(See what I mean? Easily distracted.)

"He had it narrowed down to two hundred million potential documents the last time I checked," Grayson said with a shrug. "As soon as he finds the right one, he'll e-mail it to me."

Something about the way he said it made me laugh. "You know, you really do treat Zeus like a person."

Grayson rolled his eyes.

"It's cool," I said. "Why don't you have him e-mail me, too? Or if he'd rather, he can just give me a call." I held my fingers up next to my face like a phone.

"You guys joke, but with his voice recognition soft-ware, he's totally capable of doing that," he boasted. "So don't be surprised one day when the phone rings and it's him. Let me show you."

Even though it meant postponing my homework, I slid over and let Grayson use the keyboard. He typed a quick command and started speaking to the computer.

"Zeus, notify Molly when Blue Moon search results are complete."

The computer answered in a perfectly human-sounding voice, "By text or e-mail?"

Grayson looked at me for the answer.

"Text is fine," I said with a laugh.

"Confirmed," said Zeus.

"Doesn't he need my number?" I joked.

"He already has all your contact information," Grayson said, pleased with himself and his computer.

"Maybe we should just have him solve our New Year's dilemma," I added. I turned to the computer and said, "Zeus, what are the Unlucky 13 planning to do about Blue Moon on New Year's Eve?"

Okay, so I was kidding, but Zeus didn't know that.

"Initiating search," he replied.

"Yikes," I said. "How do I tell him I was joking?"

"You don't," he said. "Zeus does not have a sense of humor. If he doesn't know the answer, he'll search for anything that has all of those keywords in it."

Before I could say anything else, the computer made a beeping noise and spoke once again. "One result."

We looked up at the main monitor and saw a freeze frame from a podcast. The funny thing is that we both recognized the person in the picture.

"Isn't that . . . ?"

". . . Action News reporter Brock Hampton," I said when Grayson couldn't place the name.

It was the same newscaster we'd eavesdropped on when he was reporting about the dead bodies discovered on Roosevelt Island and also the same one we'd seen on the Halloween broadcast talking about Jacob Blackwell's death on the subway. He was cheesy and over-the-top, which made him infinitely more interesting than the War of 1812.

"Click play," I said.

"Don't you have a ton of homework to do?" Grayson asked.

"I promise I'll get back to it in one minute and fifty-eight seconds," I said as I checked the time bar at the bottom of the video clip.

"Okay," he said.

The report wasn't really news. It was a list of special things Brock recommended to celebrate the holidays in New York. Most of it was obvious stuff like ice skating in Rockefeller Center or seeing the Christmas Spectacular at

Radio City Music Hall. But the one that caught our attention, and the one that had made it turn up in Zeus's search, was what he said about New Year's Eve.

"And what better way to celebrate the end of one year and the beginning of another than to spend New Year's Eve in Times Square," he said. "This year, I'll be there with live updates all night long, and there will be a special treat as it will be a rare blue moon. Don't be one of the unlucky ones to miss a blue moon in Times Square. It will be a night you'll never forget."

It stopped and we looked at each other.

"There's a blue moon on New Year's Eve?" I asked. "Is that weird?"

Grayson made a funny face as he thought about it. "A blue moon is just the second full moon in a month," he said. "It's almost always going to be the last day or two of the month, so that makes sense. But his phrasing at the end was really weird. Even for Brock Hampton."

He dragged the cursor back, and we watched the end again.

"Don't be one of the unlucky ones to miss a blue moon in Times Square. It will be a night you'll never forget."

"Didn't he say something about being unlucky when Jacob Blackwell's body was discovered?" Grayson asked.

I thought back and realized that's how I'd made the connection between Jacob and the Unlucky 13.

"He did. We thought it was strange then, too."

Grayson smiled, and then he started to laugh.

"What?"

"Check this out," he said. "Zeus, search Action News . . . Brock Hampton . . . unlucky."

A minute later, there were about a dozen podcast clips on the screen dating back to the beginning of the year.

Grayson smiled, and I had no idea what he was so excited about.

"This is how the undead find out," he tried to explain. "This is how they learn when and where to show up for Verify or get any other news about the Unlucky 13. They watch Brock Hampton."

We played through all of the clips, and in each one Brock used the word "unlucky" and reported on a public event. Some we already knew for sure involved the Unlucky 13. In addition to the report on the bodies discovered on Roosevelt Island and Jacob Blackwell's death on the subway, we found a story about Ulysses Blackwell's float in the Thanksgiving Parade.

"Brock's probably undead too," Grayson said. "What a perfect scam. We just think he's inept, but he's really sending secret messages to everyone in Dead City."

"Do you know what this means?" I asked.

"That we can track the Unlucky 13?" he said with a goofy smile on his face.

"Yes," I answered. "But I think it also means the undead really are planning on launching Operation Blue Moon on New Year's Eve."

Suddenly, his smile disappeared.

"You know, I think you're right."

Grayson dragged the cursor along the end of the time bar again, and we listened to Brock Hampton's final sentence one more time.

"It will be a night you'll never forget."

24

All Hands on Deck

We called Natalie and Alex and told them what we'd learned about Brock Hampton. Then it was time for Grayson to celebrate Hanukkah with his family and for me to stop talking about doing my homework and actually start doing it. I went home, shut myself in my room, and somehow managed to get it all done. It wasn't exactly my best work, but at least it didn't inflict any permanent damage to my grades. In fact, the only real harm done was to the night of sleep that got ruined by "The Tell-Tale Heart."

The story is about a murderer who hides his victim's

heart under the floorboards of his house. He then imagines that the heart comes back to life and beats so loudly that it drives him insane. It's not exactly the kind of thing you want to read just before you go to bed, right? So imagine reading it the day after you've looked into a deep freezer containing several random body parts. Needless to say, I wound up having various nightmares in which the hand, arm, leg, and finger we discovered all came back to life.

But here's the funny part: My sleeping brain was able to make a connection that my wide-awake brain totally missed. At some point during the night, it must have figured out where the body parts came from, because when I woke up, I just knew. I had suddenly put it together that Jacob Blackwell was missing an arm when his body was discovered on the subway, that Orville Blackwell lost the lower part of his leg because of the beat down Natalie gave him when we fought in the morgue, and that I chopped off Cornelius Blackwell's hand during that same fight. (The finger had fallen off it earlier.)

Theoretically, they could have been an entirely different arm, leg, hand, and finger, but I'm not a big fan of coincidence, and that seemed unlikely. The part that didn't make any sense to me, though, was why they were being preserved in the freezer. Jacob and Cornelius were both dead and would no longer have any use for their missing pieces, and Orville seemed to have transitioned quite well onto his artificial leg.

The lack of sleep caught up with me the next day, and by third period, I was dragging my way through school. I even nodded off during lunch. Lucky for me, Natalie snuck up from behind and poked me in the ribs, startling me so bad, I literally jumped out of my seat and screamed. Lucky because there might have still been a few kids left at school who weren't totally convinced I was a freak show.

"What'd you do that for?" I asked once I managed to catch my breath and regain my ability to form words.

"Sorry," she said. "It was just too perfect to pass up."

Alex and Grayson plopped down on the other side of the table and tried not to laugh too hard. Judging by the fact that everyone in the cafeteria was staring, it must have been pretty loud.

"How bad was it?" I asked.

"Not too bad," Alex said.

"No," added Grayson. "I think it's what you'd call . . . a *flinch*."

The reference to my flinch/scream on Halloween brought more laughter from the three of them. They all started digging into their lunches, and rather than defend my honor, I just laid my head back down and tried to use my backpack as a pillow.

"You've got to wake up, girl," Natalie said, poking me. Again. "Do you have your vanilla extract with you?"

"Why?" I asked. "You want to pour it on my head as a prank when I fall back asleep?"

"Tempting, but no," she answered. "I think we should save it for after school, when we're all going to the morgue."

Suddenly, I was wide awake and happy. I know that most people would think it's weird that I love going to the morgue so much. But I guess *most people* will just have to deal with the fact that the city's death house also happens to be my happy place. Go figure. The same could not be said for Grayson.

"The morgue?" he moaned. "Haven't we seen enough body parts this week?"

"You know, for a boy who likes to make fun of my flinching, you're a pretty big scaredy-cat," I teased. "The morgue's nothing. I've been hanging out there since I was seven years old."

"Yeah," said Alex. "And look how normal she turned out."

Okay, even I laughed at that one.

"Why are we going to the morgue?" Grayson asked.

"Because I contacted the Prime-O about Blue Moon and Times Square, and she wants us to go there and tell

Dr. H everything we know about it." She took a big bite out of her apple and added, "I think she's considering an all-Omega alert asking every Omega, old and new, to be in Times Square, ready to fight."

Just the thought of that was hard to fathom.

"How many Omegas would that be?" I asked.

"Maybe a hundred, a hundred and fifty," she guessed. "The Prime-O is the only one who really knows."

The addition of the morgue to my schedule and the possibility of an all-Omega alert gave me the boost of energy I needed to stay awake the rest of the school day. In fact, I was in such a good mood when we left the campus, I was willing to ride the Roosevelt Island tram. Normally, I avoid it, because, you know, it dangles from a cable above the East River. But I'd been trying to conquer my fear of heights, so when they all headed toward the subway station, I suggested, "Why don't we take the tram instead?"

They stopped in their tracks.

"The tram?" Alex asked. "The tram that runs from Roosevelt Island to Manhattan?"

"Yes," I said. "The tram."

"The tram that hangs two hundred and fifty feet in the air?" added Grayson.

"Listen, do you guys want to take it or not?" I asked as I started walking in that direction. "It'll be faster, and I know you like the view."

"You don't have to prove anything to us," Natalie said. "We can ride the subway."

"I told you guys that I'm working on my fear of heights," I said. "Besides, I have a new system."

"Does that system include an onboard anesthesiologist who is going to knock you unconscious?" Alex asked.

"You know, you really should try stand-up comedy if the whole science thing doesn't work out," I said.

"All joking aside," said Grayson. "What's your system?"

"If you must know," I admitted somewhat reluctantly, "I'm using . . . 'Endless Love.'"

Now they were really confused.

"'Endless Love' as in the eternal emotion of devotion and affection?" Grayson wondered aloud.

"No, 'Endless Love' as in the overly sappy and romantic love song from the 1980s." I told them I had come across it the day before when I was making my new playlists.

"You know how couples have a song?" I continued. "Well, 'Endless Love' was my parents' song. They danced to it on their first date and at their wedding."

Alex was trying to make sense of this. "And that somehow

makes it so you're no longer scared to dangle above the East River?"

"No, that's just an interesting part of the backstory," I said. "The reason it helps me is because it's exactly four minutes and twenty-six seconds long. That's precisely the same length as one ride on the tram."

"I'm sorry," said Alex as we reached the turnstiles. "It still doesn't make any sense to me."

"That's okay," I said, sliding my Metrocard through the reader. "It only has to make sense to me."

The big red tram car holds about one hundred people, and it was pretty full for our ride. We found a spot toward the back, and I grabbed hold of the strap that hung from the ceiling. The others were staring at me, curious as to how I was going to respond, but I was cautiously optimistic that it would work. Technically, it was just a theory. This was my first actual attempt.

"The one drawback is that I'm going to have to tune out of the conversation for the duration of the ride," I said.

I slipped my headphones on, and the instant I felt the floor beneath me rumble to life, I pressed play and cranked up the volume all the way. While everybody else was looking out the window at the approaching Manhattan skyline or down at the river below, I was in another world, listening to Lionel Richie and Diana Ross sing a duet and imagining my mom and dad slow dancing at their wedding. This way I had an idea of how far across we were without having to look. When the last note faded, I opened my eyes just as we touched down in Manhattan.

"Brilliant," said Alex, who was staring right at me.

I couldn't help myself when I responded, "I know I am, but what are you?"

Part of the reason I was so excited to go back to the morgue was that I hadn't been since the day we'd gotten suspended. I hung out there so much with my mom growing up, it felt like home and not seeing it for a few months was just odd.

My good buddy Jamaican Bob was working the guard's desk, and he flashed me a huge, toothy grin the moment he saw us. "Molly, Molly, in come free," he said playfully. "Long time no see. Wagwan?"

"That's Jamaican slang for 'What's going on?'" I explained to Grayson and Alex.

"Nothing much, just heading to an appointment with Dr. H," I answered as I put my backpack on the X-ray machine. "What's going on with you?"

"Well, now that I see you and Miss Natalie, my day is picking up," he said as he and Nat did their special six-step ritual handshake greeting.

"I don't think we introduced our two friends the last time we were here," Natalie said. "This is Alex and Grayson."

"Nice to meet you boys," he said. "Welcome to the morgue. You can call me Bob."

"Nice to meet you, Bob," Alex and Grayson said.

"And do you know what to call the dead bodies?" he asked them.

The exchanged a curious look with each other and then turned back to Bob.

"Corpses?" answered Grayson.

"No," said Bob. "You don't call them anything. They're dead, and they can't hear you anymore."

Natalie, Bob, and I all burst out laughing while Alex and Grayson shook their heads.

"It wouldn't be a trip to the morgue without one of Bob's bad jokes," I said to them as we all walked through the metal detector.

We took the elevator down to the bottom level and went to Dr. Hidalgo's lab. Right before we stepped inside, Natalie and I each swiped some vanilla extract under our noses to counteract the smell of the bodies. I offered some to the boys, and unlike our first visit they were smart enough to take me up on it.

"Is that your mom?" Grayson asked, noticing a picture on the wall.

"Yes," I said. "They put that up right after her funeral."

It was a nicely framed photograph of her in her lab coat. Underneath was a little plaque that read ROSEMARY COLLINS, FOREVER IN OUR HEARTS.

We told Dr. Hidalgo everything we knew about Blue Moon and the documents we found in M42. We even told him about the body parts in the freezer. We didn't think these were part of the same plan, but we knew that it would interest the coroner in him.

"They were stored in a mixture of ice and schist?" he said. "Fascinating."

Then we all moved over to his computer and watched some of Brock Hampton's news reports. By the time we were done, Dr. H was convinced.

"Well, looking at all of this, there are two things that I know for sure," he said.

"What?" asked Alex.

"First of all, the undead have something big planned for New Year's Eve, and we have to prepare for a worst-case scenario."

"And the other?" asked Grayson.

He looked at the four of us for a moment. "Whoever

picked you guys to work on the Baker's Dozen was pretty smart. What you've done is amazing."

Suddenly, even Grayson didn't mind being in the morgue so much. We talked a little longer, and Dr. H wrote down some notes to share with the Prime-O. He said that he'd get in touch with us once they came up with a strategy for New Year's Eve.

My lack of sleep had caught back up with me, but even though I was exhausted, I had one more thing I needed to take care of. I said good-bye to the others and took the subway up to Central Park. I walked by the zoo where I'd had my birthday party when I was five and stopped at the big clock with the dancing animals, where my mom had found me when I got lost. I had to reach her about something, and this is where she'd told me to leave her any messages.

I wrote it out on a piece of masking tape and stuck it right along the archway beneath the clock. It was written in the basic Omega code, which uses the periodic table of elements and read, "Mg/Cr O:Zn 53,58 16,19,85,68 4,90."

It wasn't about the undead. And it wasn't about the Omegas. I had promised to find a way for her to see my sister in person, and this was my plan.

Decoded, the message read, "12/24 8:30 Ice Skater Beth."

I knew Mom would know what it meant.

(A Not Particularly) Silent Night

Every Christmas Eve, Beth and I help my father with two projects at his station house. First of all, we're the servers for the big holiday feast he makes for all the firefighters who are on duty. We've known most of them forever, and it's like we're one big Italian-Irish-Polish-African-American family. They love to give Dad a hard time about anything and everything and are always looking for new ammunition. Beth gave them plenty when she told them about his mad scrapbooking skills.

"You should see how he makes the little ribbons," she said. "They're so delicate and pretty." Dad's captain, a giant man we've always called Uncle Rick, laughed so hard, he almost spit out his mashed potatoes.

Moments later, Dad walked in wearing his favorite apron—which says FIRE CHEF instead of FIRE CHIEF—and carrying a plate of turkey. Things got quiet, and all eyes turned to him.

"What's wrong?" he asked.

"I was wondering if you could help me with something," Uncle Rick said.

"Of course," he answered.

"I've been studying for my recertification test, and there's one thing I can never get straight."

"What is it?" asked Dad.

"Are you supposed to glue the pictures directly onto the scrapbook? Or should you use double-sided tape instead?"

The entire table erupted into laughter, and Dad turned two shades of red. He laughed too but quickly tried to change the subject. "So, did you catch that Jets game on Sunday? It was unbelievable, wasn't it?"

After the feast was done and all the leftovers were labeled and loaded into the refrigerator, we picked up the final donations to the station's toy drive to take them to a nearby homeless shelter.

"Michael, we left those last toys unwrapped," Uncle

Rick said to my dad. "'Cause we know you like to do the ribbon."

There were more laughs, and Dad gave Beth the stink eye as we headed out the door to go to the shelter.

It was my turn to choose family time, and since we were already going to be in the neighborhood, I decided on a night in Manhattan. The plan was to start with ice skating in Rockefeller Center and then to cross the street and go to midnight mass at St. Patrick's Cathedral.

This worked for me in so many ways. First of all, Midtown is beautiful during the holidays. There are lights and decorations everywhere, and I can't think of a better way to spend Christmas Eve.

Second, we'd learned from one of Brock Hampton's newscasts that midnight mass was going to be this year's Verify for Elias Blackwell. As my Omega team's lone Catholic member, I'd told the others that I would take care of getting a picture.

8. **Elias Blackwell**: Deceased

    Occupation: Lawyer

    Aliases: Elias Wollman, Elias Belvedere,

       Elias Olmsted

    Most Recent Home: Central Park

Role within the 13: Legal

Last Sighting: Fifth Avenue

Most important, though, I thought both of these activities gave me the perfect opportunity to include Mom as part of our holiday plans. There were plenty of places where she could watch us skate, and it would be easy for her to hide among the packed congregation in the cathedral. It wasn't exactly the same as being together, but it was as close as I could come up with.

As far as ice skating goes, the family falls into varying levels of ability. Beth is by far the most graceful. She's long and lean and took figure skating lessons when she was little. Dad played hockey in high school. He's the fastest, although it's not particularly pretty to look at. He also has a tendency to slam into people—and by "people," I mean me—like he's playing for the Stanley Cup. Meanwhile, I'm the worst. (I know, shocker!) I do what Dad calls "the Molly shuffle" and never stray more than a few inches from the safety of the side rail that wraps around the rink. Despite this lack of skill, I really enjoy going once or twice a year. I especially love skating at Rockefeller Center, where you're outside, surrounded by the city, and right beneath the massive seventy-five-foot-tall Christmas tree.

After going around for a few laps without spotting Mom, I began to worry that she didn't see my message. I was scanning faces in the crowd when Dad came to a hockey stop right in front of me. But because I was looking up instead of where I was going, I slammed right into him, and we had to scramble to keep our balance.

"Dad?!" I said, exasperated. "You almost tackled me."

"Tackling is football," he said. "In hockey, they call it 'checking.'"

"Well, I'll make sure to use the right term when I try to explain to the doctor how I broke my hand . . . again."

"Besides, you were the one who wasn't watching where you were going," he said. "Who are you looking for?"

Busted.

I stammered for a moment, trying to come up with an answer. "Hockey scouts," I said. "You know, from the Rangers or the Islanders, in case they're looking for a middle-aged player with good paramedic skills."

He smiled and waved a finger at me. "Don't forget the Devils," he said. "I could handle a commute into Jersey to play professional hockey."

We skated around together for a little bit and talked about nothing in particular. It was nice and relaxed. We both looked over at Beth, who was gliding effortlessly across the middle of the rink. Her bright pink jacket made it impossible to miss her. If Mom was up there somewhere, I'm sure she was glued to her every move.

"I want you to be honest with me about something," he said.

"Of course," I answered, nervous about where this could go.

"Did the thing about scrapbooking just slip out? Or did she sell me out on purpose?"

I laughed. "You know the answer to that one."

"That's what I figured," he said as he focused in on her. "I think it's time for a little revenge."

"You're not going to tackle her, are you?"

He gave me a frustrated look. "It's *check*, not tackle. How many times do I have to go over that? And of course not. I'm going to do something much worse than that. I'm going to embarrass her in front of those boys she's flirting with."

Sure enough, there were a group of high school boys watching her closely. She wasn't exactly skating with them, but she was staying close and maintaining just enough eye contact to keep them in her orbit, not unlike Jupiter does with its many moons.

Of course, Jupiter gets by with gravity and doesn't have to worry about a dad getting in the way. Ours skated right up and did his hockey-stop thing and almost knocked one of the boys to the ground. Then he started giving her encouragement.

"Looking good, Beth!" he said loud enough so I could easily hear him all the way on the edge. "You're burnin' so bright, you're going to melt the ice."

As if that weren't cringe-worthy enough, he turned to the boys and said, "I'm her dad. I used to play hockey in school, and I'm thinking about getting back into it. You know any leagues around here for guys my age?"

They were gone before he finished his question.

"Guess that's a no," he said, turning toward Beth. "It's just you and me now."

"All right, I shouldn't have mentioned the scrapbooking," she said. "I apologize."

"Good. Consider this your first Christmas present, a little gift I like to call sweet revenge," he said. "And, fitting for this weather, it's a dish best served cold."

The ice skating rink is located on the lower plaza of Rockefeller Center so that if you're on the street level, you look down on it. That's where I finally spied Mom on my next lap. She had tucked herself into a little spot near the Christmas tree and blended right in with the crowd. We locked eyes long enough so that she'd know that I'd seen her, and then she flashed me a smile that was the best present I could ask for.

As far as skating goes, I was starting to get the hang of it and actually went about fifteen feet without holding on to anything when I got slammed into the rail. Again.

"C'mon, Dad," I said, a little frustrated. "I get the point. It's called a *check*, not a tackle."

Except, when I turned around, it wasn't my dad.

She was a big, orange-and-yellow-toothed Level 3 zombie. She squeezed my forearm so tight, my fingers tingled, and she pressed me against the rail long enough so that she could sniff me like an animal and get my scent. I looked up to where I'd seen my mother, and she was already gone, no doubt on her way to rescue me.

Instinctively, I tried a Jeet Kune Do move, not thinking about the fact that they weren't exactly designed with ice skates in mind. Instead of kicking Zelda Zombie, I wound up slamming butt-first into the ice.

I looked up at her and considered my situation, which was quickly spinning out of control. I had to defeat a zombie . . . on ice skates . . . without attracting the attention of my father and sister . . . and without them seeing my undead mother. There was simply no way this could get worse.

Then it got worse.

As I struggled to get back up onto my skates, I saw none other than Natalie skating right toward me. And she was angry.

I braced to be slammed into the railing one more time. But Natalie being Natalie, she of course stopped with the precision of an Olympic ice dancer inches from my face.

"Who are you sending messages to?"

I didn't know who to deal with first: Natalie or the zombie. I checked to see that my dad and Beth were busy, so that was good, but I still had no idea where my mom was.

"What are you talking about?" I asked her.

Just then, Zelda Zombie took a wild swipe at me, and I had to duck to miss it, which almost made me fall again.

"I mean, haven't your secrets already gotten us in enough trouble?" Natalie asked.

"I still don't know what you're talking about, and I'm kind of in the middle of something here," I said as I scrambled to keep my balance. "So, either you can be more specific, or you can help me fight this girl without my dad and sister finding out."

"I saw the coded message in Central Park," she said. "It led me here to you. Who was it written for?"

While she was talking, Zelda grabbed me by the

shoulders and pushed. With skates on, I had no way to stop, and I just slid in reverse and braced to slam into either the ice or the railing. But someone caught me from behind and lifted me just as I was about to hit the ice. I looked up and saw her face.

"Mom," I said out loud before I realized it.

"Mom?" Natalie asked, looking at me and then at her.

With me in her arms, my mother had nowhere to go. She looked up at Natalie and smiled. "Hi."

Zelda, of course, was still determined to take me out, and as I looked back, I saw that my father and sister were about to turn the corner and come right at us.

"Beth, Dad, zombie," I said to the two of them, hoping they could do the math on their own.

Natalie thought for a second and nodded.

"Got it."

She did an axel or spin or whatever you call it and clipped Zelda in the backs of her thighs with her skate, knocking her right into my mother's arm. Mom spun around, taking Zelda with her, and by the time Dad and Beth got to me, everything appeared normal.

"We should probably head over to mass," Dad said. "It's going to get pretty crowded in there."

"Great idea," I answered.

I shuffled off with them, and neither had any idea that they were just a few feet from Mom. I'd just have to trust that she and Natalie could take care of Zelda and figure out a way to deal with Natalie knowing about Mom.

As far as church goes, I don't really love going to services all that much. I think my time in Catholic school kind of burned me out. But I've always loved midnight mass, especially singing all the carols. It started with "O Come All Ye Faithful" and ended with "Joy to the World," two of my favorites.

I managed to use my phone to sneak a couple of pictures of Elias Blackwell, who was actually one of the readers. He spent much of the mass sitting with the archbishop, and I couldn't figure out how he managed to get such a prominent spot. I later learned that he's a big donor to the church and often provides free legal services for some of its charities.

Apparently, Natalie and Mom were able to take care of everything, because halfway through the service, I got a text from Natalie that simply read, "All good." (I also got a dirty look from my dad for checking a message during church.) And as I was walking from my seat to communion, I saw my mother in the crowd. I was able to pick a line that went right by her, and as I did, I put my hand on the pew in front of her. She put her hand on mine and said, "Merry Christmas, Molly."

"Merry Christmas, Mom," I said as I held her hand for an instant longer.

She was crying, but I'm pretty sure they were tears of joy.

Countdown (We Return to Where the Story Began)

The week between Christmas and New Year's was surprisingly quiet. Once I got the pictures of Elias Blackwell at St. Patrick's, there wasn't really anything else for us to do Baker's Dozen–wise. And as for Blue Moon and New Year's Eve, we were still waiting for instructions to come from the Prime-O.

Christmas Day started in Queens with Beth and Dad; moved on to Brooklyn, where Grandma and Grandpa Collins called me Little Molly Bear about a thousand times; and ended in northern New Jersey, where we had dinner and opened presents with Grandma and Grandpa

Bigelow and slept in the same house where my dad grew up. That night, it snowed, and we spent the next morning sledding down a hill on cookie sheets. It was a total blast.

A couple days later, I was finally able to meet up with Natalie and talk about my mom. Her parents were having some sort of ritzy dinner party so she snuck out and met me at a pizza place close to her house.

"I'm guessing your big secret is that your mother is undead," she said.

I nodded, unsure what her mood was like, but I was relieved when she smiled.

"That certainly explains a lot. When did you find out?"

"On the bridge with Marek," I said. "She saved my life."

"Wow," Natalie said, taking it all in. "Just wow."

I could tell she was running through the time line of events in her head. "Was she the one who picked us for Baker's Dozen?"

"Yep."

"I can understand why you didn't tell us."

I was ready for there to be a "but," some kind of angry admonition, but there wasn't. She just said, "Well, you don't have to worry about me telling anyone. Your secret's certainly safe with me."

Then the most unexpected thing happened. Natalie started to cry. She really didn't want to, but the more she tried to stop it, the worse it got.

"What's the matter?" I asked.

At first she said it was nothing. But I pushed and after she thought about it for a long while she said, "I'm going to tell you a story that I've never told anyone."

"I think we're beyond the point of keeping secrets from each other."

She smiled and nodded her agreement as she still tried to keep her emotions under control.

"A few years ago, we were at the country club, and I was horseback riding while my parents played golf. It's something we'd done a million times. Just a normal Saturday. Except this time, I got thrown from my horse and was knocked unconscious."

"Oh no," I said.

"It was terrifying. Everything turned out okay, but for about an hour it was bad. I've never been so scared in my life. And the thing that helped me through it, the thing that gave me strength, was the look of concern on my father's face as he checked to make sure I wasn't having any side effects from the concussion. I'll never forget that look. I remember thinking it must be the same look he gives his patients before he operates. It just made me feel safe and cared for."

"That's . . . really nice," I said.

"I'm not finished," she said, trying to keep from crying more. "Later, as we rode back into the city, I found the scorecard from their game . . . and when I looked at it . . . I realized that they finished playing their round before they came to check on me."

I couldn't believe this was possibly true. I stared in stunned amazement for a moment. "You don't know that," I said, hoping I was right. "They might have already been done by the time they found out you'd gotten hurt."

"No," she said, the tears falling again. "I asked them, and they admitted it. They weren't even embarrassed by it. They said that they knew I was in good hands and explained that Dad was having one of the best rounds of his life. So they played the last two holes, and *then* they came to check on me."

She looked right into my eyes, and her expression broke my heart. I didn't know what to say.

"Your mother literally came back from the dead to help you, and my parents couldn't even be bothered to interrupt a golf game."

We sat quietly for a while until the server brought our

pizza. We hung out for a few hours, and by the time I left her, she was actually laughing and having a good time. But it still broke my heart, and I would never have guessed that the girl with the luxury life on Central Park West would envy anything about my cramped Queens existence?

Our New Year's Eve assignment came on December 30. We were told that there was an all-Omega alert due to a credible threat from the undead against the living.

Even though we knew it was coming, there was something about reading it that took my breath away. There was no telling how big this could get. Our team was assigned to the Rockefeller Center subway station and told to separate and follow any Level 2s heading for Times Square.

That's how I wound up tailing the hipster couple I told you about at the beginning of the story. Now it's about an hour and a half before midnight, and I'm still barricaded in right behind them. I've thought back through everything that's happened since Halloween, but it still seems like there's a missing piece that I'm just not seeing.

I'm not exactly sure where the other members of my team are, but we have been texting back and forth, trying to lighten the mood with some humor.

According to Liberty, Marek's Verify won't officially begin until the stroke of midnight. Once he doesn't show, however, there's no telling what will happen. The real fear is that when everyone starts counting down the final sixty seconds of the year and the crystal ball goes down the flagpole, it might also be signaling the beginning of an all-out war with the undead. At that point, one of the other Unlucky 13—my money's still on Ulysses—could step forward and claim control of Dead City. Then, in his first act as mayor, he could order Operation Blue Moon into full effect.

My phone buzzes, and I check to see which teammate is sending me a text. I laugh out loud when I read that it's not from any of them. Believe it or not, it's from Zeus. Grayson had instructed his computer to alert me when it finished its search of the CIA database, and it's doing just that.

"Hi, Molly. Here is the report. Zeus."

Okay, there aren't any abbreviations or emoticons, so it doesn't feel like an text from an actual person, but it's still pretty impressive. The band that's currently onstage isn't particularly good, so I decide to go ahead and read the file.

According to the CIA, the mission's original plan was to see how many New Yorkers would have to be converted to communism in order to change public opinion of the Soviet Union. Our worry is that the undead are using the same strategy, except rather than converting people to communism, they're planning on changing them into zombies. Now Zeus has sent me the CIA's conclusions, which had been ripped out of the file.

I start to read them, and they aren't at all what I expected. Apparently, the experts concluded that it would be completely impractical to convert so many people to anything. This makes me smile. Hopefully, the undead reached the same conclusion, and we're all just out here with nothing to worry about.

But as I continue to read, I come across a passage that's alarming. The experts also concluded that it would be much easier to reach the same goal by simply converting a few powerful people who could help shape public opinion.

If the Unlucky 13 wanted to do something like that, they would have to infect community leaders and turn them into zombies. I mull this over for a while. I think back to the first Verify, when we saw Ulysses Blackwell riding in the Thanksgiving Day parade. He spent hours standing next to the chief of police. Then I consider the most recent Verify at St. Patrick's. Elias Blackwell spent the entire mass sitting with the archbishop. Suddenly, it starts to make sense.

I pull a folded sheet of paper out of my pocket and

look at the schedule of events for the night. At midnight, the ball is going to drop when the mayor of New York pushes a plunger on the stage.

I finally see the puzzle pieces that I've been missing.

The chief of police. The archbishop. The mayor.

The undead aren't infecting a million New Yorkers; they're getting revenge against the three wise men. The actual men are different, but their positions are still just as powerful today as they were in 1896. If those three men become undead, the Unlucky 13 will be able to start building the power it has always craved. I start to hyperventilate.

At midnight, one of the Unlucky 13 will appear on the stage with the mayor of New York. When he's there, he'll become the new leader of Dead City and will infect one of the most powerful people in the country.

Unless I can stop him first.

Ω 27

Two Zombie Mayors

As soon as I figure out what's happening, I send a text to the rest of my team and tell them that we need to have an emergency meeting in front of the New York Public Library. I pick the library because we need to find one another as fast as possible, and it's the closest landmark I can think of that might not be overrun by tourists. I also send a quick text alerting Dr. H so he can pass the info along to the Prime-O. I'm not going to make the same mistakes I've made before. I don't have time to give many details, but I want them to know that we're on the move.

Getting out of my spot in the crowd turns out to be harder than I expect. Luckily, I'm small enough that I'm able to push and squeeze and crawl around and under all of the people and barricades until I finally break free of the mob. As soon as I do, I start sprinting toward the library. Even though the temperature has dipped into the thirties, I'm running so hard that I start sweating inside my jacket.

When I get there, I find Alex anxiously pacing back and forth between the two lion statues that stand in front of the library's entrance. He hurries down the flight of stairs and comes right up to me. His eyes are full of frustration as he says, "You know we've lost our spots, right?"

"Yes, I know," I answer, trying to calm him like it's no big deal.

"I was right in the middle of the crowd next to some mean-looking Level 2s, and I had a good view of the stage," he continues. "Now that place is gone for good. I can't get back there."

"It's okay," I assure him. "That's not where we need to be."

"Really? Because I thought the whole plan was for all the Omegas to be spread throughout the crowd in Times Square so that we can fight back once the zombies start to attack."

"They're not going to attack the crowd," I tell him, hoping that I've got this figured out correctly. "They're only going to attack one person."

Before I can elaborate, Natalie comes up from the corner of Fifth and Forty-Second, taking long angry strides, with Grayson a few yards behind her, trying to keep up.

"What's the emergency?" she demands, her mood mirroring Alex's. "Because I was in a good position to take out four Level 2s. Four of them. And now they're all alone, with no one to stop them when they get the order to attack."

Oddly, in the middle of all this, it dawns on me that even though they're mad about it, they still came. All of them came. They trust me that much, and that trust means everything to me. Of course, now I have to prove that I deserve it.

"Stop complaining and listen to me!" I exclaim, hoping a little intensity will quiet them for a moment. "We need to change the plan because the undead aren't going to attack the people in the crowd."

"And why do you say that?"

I hold up my phone with the text from Zeus. It's not like they can read it with me waving it around, but it's the only prop I have.

"Because Operation Blue Moon isn't about infecting

as many people as possible," I try to explain. "It's about infecting a small but important group of people. Three, to be exact."

"Three?" says Alex. He's confused, but he's starting to listen. "Why three instead of a million?"

"It started back at Thanksgiving," I say. "That's when they infected the chief of police. Then on Christmas Eve, they infected the archbishop. Tonight, they're planning to infect . . ."

". . . the mayor!" Grayson says, putting it all together.

I point directly at him. "That's exactly right. Tonight they want to infect the mayor." (I admit that having someone else reach the same conclusion makes me feel a whole lot more confident.)

"But why?" Natalie asks, shaking her head. "What does that give them?"

"It gives them power and revenge," I answer.

"What revenge?"

"Revenge against the three wise men," I say. "Revenge against the men who ruined their lives."

"But the three wise men are long dead," Alex responds.

"Maybe so, but the positions that they held are still important and powerful," I remind him.

"And if the current people in those positions are

undead," Grayson continues, "it will bring that power and influence to the Unlucky 13. Both above- and below-ground."

"Think about it," I say. "Think about what it would be like if there are two zombie mayors. One for New York and one for Dead City."

Just the concept of that quiets us for a moment as we contemplate the dangers that could result from such a situation.

"That would be very, very bad," Natalie says, coming around. "But what can we do? It's already after eleven. That means we've got less than an hour to warn the mayor, who happens to be surrounded by a million screaming people at the biggest party in the world."

"Do we have any idea where he is?" I ask. "Has anyone seen him tonight?"

"I did," Alex says. "He was already on the stage, doing a television interview."

The stage was built right at One Times Square, the old skyscraper that used to be home to the *New York Times*. This is where the crystal ball has dropped every year since the newspaper started the tradition in 1907.

"And that's where he'll be at midnight when he presses the plunger to make the ball fall," Grayson adds.

"Is there any way we can charge the stage?" I ask, even though I'm pretty sure I know the answer.

"No," Alex replies with a chuckle. "In addition to the million people in the crowd, there are also police everywhere. We'd never get within a hundred feet."

"We've got to think outside the box," Natalie says as she starts to pace. "We've got to be creative."

"I know," offers Grayson. "Let's play One Foot Trivia."

Natalie looks at him and frowns. "That's not what I meant," she moans. "This is serious."

"I *am* being serious," he says as he lifts one foot in the air and begins to balance. "We always answer the hard questions when we play One Foot Trivia. Maybe it will help us find the right answer if we play now. Who's with me?"

"Not me," says Alex, shaking his head. "Games aren't going to help us any."

I go to shoot down the idea too, but then I think about the fact that everyone trusted me when it seemed like an unwise thing to do. I figure the least I can do for Grayson is return the favor.

"I'll play," I say to him. "I'll try anything that might help."

"Thanks," he says. "The category is Times Square."

I lift my left foot and look him right in the eye. "Go."

"How do you get to One Times Square without actually going through Times Square?" he asks.

I wobble for a moment and start brainstorming. "Helicopter?"

"Won't work," he replies. "We couldn't get one, and even if we could, we wouldn't be able to navigate through all the buildings and land there."

"Come on, guys," Natalie says frustrated. "You're wasting time."

"I don't see you coming up with any answers on two feet," Grayson says defensively. "Keep trying, Molly."

Natalie and Alex have had enough. They turn away and start pacing again, but I'm sticking with it. As I try to keep my balance, I wobble some more and almost put my second foot down. I have to bend over to keep from falling, and when I do, I get a glimpse of a newspaper vending machine. Something about it catches my attention. It's the *New York Times*. Suddenly, my brain races back to the last flatline party we crashed, and much to my surprise, I come up with the answer.

"You go underground and enter through the giant room with all the old printing presses left over by the *New York Times*!" I practically shout, thrilled with the realization. "Just like we did when we crashed the flatline party."

The others all turn to me with amazed expressions.

"That would work," says Alex. "That would absolutely work!"

Natalie goes over to Grayson and gives him three quick high fives. "I take it all back. I freaking love One Foot Trivia."

"I know," he says, beaming. "It's amazing. There's nothing it can't do."

When we crashed the flatline party, we got there by using the trapdoor inside of the Times Square subway station. But Alex points out a problem. "Times Square station is closed on New Year's."

"That's right," says Natalie. "I forgot about that."

Grayson smiles.

"But Bryant Park is open," he says. "We can go underground there and sneak over to Times Square through the walkway that connects the stations. And since the station's closed, there won't be any people on the platform when we want to use the trapdoor."

No one says another word. There's no time. We just start racing toward the Bryant Park subway station.

"What time is it?" I ask between heavy breaths as we reach the entrance.

"Eleven eleven," Natalie answers without breaking stride. "We've got forty-nine minutes."

The Power of the Press

There are a couple of transit cops we have to avoid, but since they're watching a small television broadcasting the New Year's celebration, we're able to slip by them and move unnoticed into the Times Square station. We hurry past the darkened Spanish music shop and down two flights of stairs before we make it to the southbound platform. Just as Grayson predicted, there's not a person in sight. Alex lifts the trapdoor, and we silently disappear down into Dead City.

"I forgot how ugly this place is," Natalie says as she scans the abandoned tunnels that run beneath the station. There's trash and graffiti everywhere. And lots of rats. I can't see them, but I can hear them scurrying along by my feet.

I try to block the image of the megarodents out of my mind and ask, "Does anyone remember the way?"

"We followed the music from the party," Alex says. "Unfortunately, there's not a flatline party again tonight."

"No," Natalie says with a grin. "But there *is* music. Listen."

We listen for a moment, and sure enough, we can make out the faint echoes of a rock-and-roll song playing in the distance. It's coming from the band performing live on the stage in Times Square. All we have to do is follow it, and it will lead us right where we want to go.

"Remember, we're not the only ones who'll be coming this way," Alex reminds us. "Any zombies coming from Dead City are going to take this same route."

We try to move quickly while still being careful, but it's not easy because the tunnel is so dark. We all hold our phones out so that they cast some light ahead of us, and we keep following the music, which gets louder as we get closer.

"There it is," Grayson says, pointing toward a doorway ahead of us. "I remember that sign."

Sure enough, there's an old metal sign with faded lettering that reads NEW YORK TIMES.

"I remember it too," I say. "We're almost there."

Once we reach the door, we pick up the pace and hurry through a series of hallways as the music continues to get louder and louder until we step out into the massive printing press room.

"Found it!" I say with a proud swagger as Natalie and I share a fist bump.

The room is two levels high, and even though there are security lights hanging from the ceiling, they're barely bright enough to illuminate such a large area. The lights sway back and forth and cast twisted shadows across the hulking presses.

"Eleven thirty-five," Natalie says, checking the time on her phone. "We've only got twenty-five minutes to get up to the stage and warn the mayor."

"Yeah . . . about that," a voice says from in front of us. "I think we're going to have to say . . . no on warning anybody."

Just then a bank of much brighter lights turns on and floods the area. I have to blink a few times for my eyes to adjust, but when they finally focus, I see none other than Ulysses Blackwell standing in our way. The banker who once wore ugly polyester suits is now dressed for success in an expensive business suit, a red power tie, and a thick charcoal gray overcoat.

"It looks like someone's running for mayor of Dead City," I whisper to the others.

It would be one thing if Ulysses was alone, but he's flanked by a rather imposing collection of Level 2 thugs, including his bodyguard cousins Orville and Edmund.

"Eleven," Alex says, giving us a quick headcount.

"Which is much more than four," Ulysses interjects. "You see, I work with numbers, so I can tell you that the math doesn't really work in your favor. That puts you in a bit of a rough spot."

"He's right," I say to the others. "Any suggestions?"

Alex barely moves his lips as he whispers a one-word answer. "Stall."

At first I don't get it, but then I realize what he's thinking. If we can keep Ulysses busy past midnight, we can keep him from appearing at Verify and taking over Dead City. I think back to when I had to stall the security guard at the Flatiron Building. Like it or not, it turns out that I'm the team's "staller." The trick is to talk first and talk fast to try to control the conversation.

"You know, we've never formally met," I say, stepping forward. "You're Ulysses, right?"

"Nice try, but I don't really have time for chitchat." He turns to his cousin. "Orville, you want to take care of this?"

Orville flashes a terrifying grin of crooked orange-and-yellow teeth, many of which are broken in half. He starts to limp my way. But he's not really coming at me. Instead, he's focused on Natalie behind me. He no doubt wants to finish what he started the last time they fought. I know that if that happens, Alex will jump in, and there'll be no stopping the battle from playing out. With eleven against four, we'll be finished in minutes, and Ulysses will have plenty of time to get to Verify.

I decide to try option number two.

"And you're Orville," I say, trying to intercept him. "You know, we don't need to fight. There's no reason why the living and the undead cannot work together. All we have to do is . . ."

Orville doesn't even wait for me to finish. He just reaches down, picks me up, and throws me against a rusted old printing press. My body makes a pair of loud thud noises. The first is when I hit the press, and the second is when I crumple to the floor.

As much as I'd like to lie on the floor and moan, I see Alex start to make a move toward him, and I bounce back on my feet.

"No!" I call out forcefully, trying to keep the fight from beginning. "Orville and I are just negotiating. I made a suggestion, and he rejected it. Now I'm going to make a counteroffer."

I'm more than a little woozy, but I somehow manage to stagger toward him. I check my watch, there are still twenty-two minutes left until midnight. I don't know how many times I can take getting thrown through the air. But at the current rate we're going, that would take a lot more *thuds*.

"Seriously," I say, offering Orville a handshake. "We can do this peacefully."

Once again, Orville picks me up and holds me high in the air. Then, just as he's about to throw me for a second time, a woman's voice calls down from above.

"I would suggest putting her down . . . gently," she says. "Consider that a warning."

All eyes move to the metal catwalk that winds through the printing presses on the upper level.

"Is that who I think it is?" gasps Grayson.

"Yep," I call to him. "It's my mom."

"But how . . . ?"

"It's kind of a long story," I say, cutting off the questions for now.

"I'm sorry," Ulysses interrupts, turning to my mother. "My cousin Orville's not much of a talker, but I'm curious:

What kind of warning are you giving us?"

"A simple one so you'll be sure to understand it with your tiny zombie brains," she says with badass confidence. "If you mess with my daughter, you mess with me."

Ulysses laughs and goes to say something else, but she cuts him off and continues talking.

"And if you mess with her team, you mess with mine."

Suddenly, a host of past Omegas start to step out from the shadows and behind the printing presses. I don't know if it's my mother's actual team or just people she pulled together from all the Omegas in the crowd, but there are eight or nine in total. I recognize some of the faces, like Dr. H and Liberty, but am totally surprised by others like Jamaican Bob, the security guard from the morgue. None, however, is more surprising than the man who walks right up to Orville: a man who hasn't left Roosevelt Island in decades.

"Dr. Gootman?!" I say, surprised.

"Actually," he replies, "for tonight, I prefer Milton."

Orville drops me to the floor (thud number three, but still a welcome development), and he turns to face the cousin he hasn't seen in more than a century.

"Hello, Orville," Milton says. "Edmund, Ulysses. It's been a long time."

"You have no business being here," Ulysses thunders as he storms over to him.

"Well," Milton replies, refusing to back down, "you have no business trying to hurt these children."

The two of them stand face-to-face for a brief but tense moment until Alex walks over and interrupts by tapping Ulysses on the shoulder.

"By the way," he says, "when you add in the new people, the math turns out to be pretty good for us."

Without hesitation, Alex throws a punch that sends Ulysses sprawling across the floor and then moves right at Orville.

"You're pretty good at beating up girls," he says. "But how are you with guys closer to your own size?"

Orville and Alex grab each other, and within seconds, the entire room bursts into a rumble. It's like nothing I've ever seen before as little pockets of action erupt all around me. I see my mom leap down from the catwalk and start throwing punches at Edmund while Liberty joins Alex in fighting Orville.

Ulysses gets up from the floor, and the moment he realizes that he's lost control of the situation, he tries to make a run for it toward Times Square. He's cut off by Grayson and Jamaican Bob, who make a rather unique pair. Neither of them is actually fighting much, but they still manage to trap Ulysses in between two printing presses.

I'm so swept up in the action that's unfolding in front of me that I don't notice the zombie who comes up from behind and knocks me into the printing press. (That's one thud too many.)

"You got lucky there," I say, rubbing my jaw as I get up. "But that luck's about to change."

I charge at him and pull out some of my best Jeet Kune Do moves. He has no idea how to fight back and after three fake outs, he leaves me an opening, and I land a punch that knocks him out cold. I'm about to go in for the kill when I hear it.

The scream belongs to Natalie, and it's bloodcurdling.

I leave the zombie and race over to where she is. I find her unconscious on the floor, one trail of blood trickling from her nose and another from her mouth.

"Natalie!" I cry out.

I look and see that Edmund is the one who had done this. He's sneering down at the two of us, his red hair wild and his eyes burning orange. I get up to fight him, but I never get the chance. Instead, Alex swoops in from out of nowhere and dismantles him with the most furious attack I've ever seen. It could be a commercial for

Krav Maga. Edmund never even gets a single punch off.

When the flurry ends, Alex steps back, and Edmund's dead body falls to the floor in a heap.

Both of us rush back to help Natalie, but Dr. H and my mother are already tending to her. They're both excellent doctors, so that's a relief, but I can't tell how serious her injuries are. She keeps opening and closing her eyes, trying to focus.

"What time?" she asks.

It seems like an odd question, but I look at my watch and answer, "Eleven fifty."

Finally, her eyes find me and open wide. She's fading in and out but manages to say two words: "Verify . . . Milton."

It takes me a moment to put it together, but when I realize what she means, I begin to nod. "That's brilliant, Natalie. That is brilliant."

"What?" asks Mom.

I look around and see that most of the zombies, including Orville and Ulysses, have run into the darkness of Dead City. With Edmund dead, the only member of the Unlucky 13 left is Milton.

"If we can get Milton to Verify," I say to her, "he'll take charge of Dead City. He'll become the new mayor."

Realizing that I've gotten the message, Natalie flashes a blood-smeared smile and passes out.

"Is she okay?"

"Yes," Dr. H assures me. "She just needs to rest."

"You take him," Mom says to me. "Get Milton on the stage."

I look down at my best friend, bleeding and unconscious. I think about her parents playing golf when she was injured. "I can't leave her," I say. "Someone else can take him."

"We're doctors, Molly, we'll take care of her." I realize she's right.

"Dr. Goot—I mean, Milton—we better hurry." I turn to the boys. "Come on, we might need some help."

The four of us race out of the printing press room and then out of One Times Square. The stage is right in front of us, and as we're heading there, I try to figure out a plan of attack.

"How do we do this?" I ask. "How do we make sure people see him?"

We scan the stage and are almost blinded by the lights of a row of television cameras.

"Action News reporter Brock Hampton," says Grayson. "He's the one who confirms all the Verifies. He said he'd be up here broadcasting all night long. Even a reporter as bad as he is will jump at the chance to have the first-ever interview with Milton Blackwell."

"Perfect," I say. "Let's find him."

There are only a couple of minutes left before midnight, and the crowd is buzzing with excitement.

"There he is!" Alex calls out, pointing toward one of the reporters doing an interview. "He's interviewing the mayor."

I try to give Milton instructions as we hurry across the stage. "All right, you've got to do an interview with Brock Hampton."

"But the undead don't know who I am," he says, raising his voice so that he can be heard over the all the noise.

"They don't know what you look like," I reply. "But they *definitely* know who you are. Just look into the camera and tell everyone that your name's Milton Blackwell and see what happens from there."

We reach the interview site right as Brock is finishing with the mayor.

"It's really going to be an amazing year," the mayor says. "And so much of the credit belongs to my good friend here."

The mayor motions to someone off to his side and asks

him to join him on camera. The man moves awkwardly, as though he's not fully coordinated. The mayor puts his arm around him and talks directly into the camera. "Here's someone that you're really going to hear from in the upcoming year. He's amazing, and his name is Marek Blackwell."

As he steps into the light from the camera, I see that it really is Marek. He seems bent and broken, but there's no denying that it's him. The blood drains from my face, and I feel like I might faint.

"Now, I've got to take care of some business," the mayor says with a laugh as he walks off camera.

There's less than a minute until midnight, and the entire crowd is counting down the final seconds of the year. Alex, Grayson, and Milton all look to me, and I have no answer. I have no idea how Marek is standing before us.

"Do you have anything you want to say?" Brock asks him as he puts the microphone in front of him.

"I will in a few seconds," Marek replies as the countdown reaches ten.

He turns our way and seems genuinely surprised that we're there. He smiles a wicked grin, and I see that his teeth have yellowed even more.

Then I notice his left hand. It's missing the ring finger,

just like his brother Cornelius. I see that he has trouble using the hand, and it dawns on me that it isn't just like Cornelius's hand. It actually *is* Cornelius's hand. As the countdown reaches five, he tries to pose for the camera, and I can tell that his leg is bent in an unnatural direction.

I think about the body parts we discovered in the freezer and realize what's happened. He has Cornelius's hand . . . and Orville's leg . . . and Jacob's arm. I turn to the others.

"They've rebuilt him," I say, trying to be heard over the crowd. I look right at Milton and shake my head. "They've rebuilt him with the body parts of your brothers and cousins."

The countdown reaches zero, and a million people scream, blow horns, cheer, and make noise.

Calmly on the stage, Marek looks right at me and winks. Then he turns to the camera and says, "Happy New Year," verifying his still-strong hold on the world of the undead.